FANTASY KIT

FANTASY KIT

Adam McOmber

www.blacklawrence.com

Executive Editor: Diane Goettel
Cover Design: Matthew Revert
Book Design: Amy Freels

ISBN: 978-1-62557-140-3

Published 2022 by Black Lawrence Press.

For Brian Leung

Contents

For Witches

Ohio, 1994

Here is a language for witches. No. Here is a language for high school. No. Here is magic in all its occult guises. No. Here is high school in all its occult guises. No. Here is a hallway in a high school. The floor is gray linoleum. Lockers line the walls. On the doors of some of the lockers are footballs cut from construction paper. Jersey numbers are written on the footballs in black felt-tip marker. At the end of the hall is a banner that reads: "Go Bobcats!" A bobcat with black ears and yellow eyes is painted in one corner of the banner. No. Here is a path in the forest at midnight. The path is lined with gray trees. Nailed to the trunks of the trees are the long dark tongues of cows. The tongues were removed from the animals with a knife. At the far end of the path is a banner with a symbol drawn on it. No. Here is a high school student named Tom. He lives in a small town in Ohio. For the past three years, Tom has been in love with his best friend, Jason, who plays football. Jason has no idea Tom is gay. Or maybe he has an idea. But it doesn't matter. Tom wishes there were some spell or even a curse that would make Jason fall in love with him. No. Here is a figure in the forest. The figure passes through the trees, touching the bloodied cow tongues with the tips of its fingers. No. Tom stands in the bathroom of the high school and looks at his face in the mirror. He supposes it is a handsome face. He supposes that doesn't matter. No. Here is a figure crawling like a horror on a path between the trees. No. Here is Tom waiting for Jason after football practice. Usually, they walk home together, but Jason has been more distant lately. They're both going to be seniors next year. No. Here is Tom walking home alone. No. Here are all the trees in the forest attempting to speak with their cow tongues. Blood runs from the tongues as they twitch and curl. No. Here is a hallway in a high school. Someone has torn down all the paper footballs and thrown them on the floor. Someone has torn down the banner too. Ripped it in half. The bobcat stares at the ceiling with vacant yellow eyes. No. Here are the voices calling. They are not the voices of the trees. They are not the voices of the cows. They are the voices of other things. Disembodied. Moving through darkness. And they speak, all at once, in a language no one has ever heard before.

There's Someone at the Door

Barbara is reading a novel.

It's Sunday, just after nine p.m.

Her husband enters the living room, drying his hands on a dishcloth. He says: "There's someone at the door."

Barbara lowers the novel. She looks at her husband.

"I heard a knock," he says.

"I didn't hear anything," Barbara says. She lifts a glass of wine from the table beside her chair and takes a sip.

"Well, you weren't listening then," her husband says.

But Barbara has been listening. She's quite sensitive to sound. And she would know if someone knocked on the door, especially if her husband heard it all the way from the kitchen.

Now her husband is walking toward the foyer, as if he means to answer the door.

Barbara considers the fact that her husband might be pulling some kind of prank. He used to do that sort of thing when they first met. They were in college then. He sat behind her in astronomy class. Every time she turned around, he was smiling, as if he knew some secret.

Barbara's husband reaches the front door and begins to unfasten the chain.

"Wait," Barbara says. She doesn't know why she tells him to wait, other than the fact that it simply doesn't seem right to answer a door if no one has knocked.

Her husband pauses, turning to look at her. "Wait for what?"

"I don't know," Barbara says. "Just—"

"What if it's Mrs. Miller?" her husband asks.

Barbara considers this. Mrs. Miller is their neighbor. Her husband died in a car accident years ago. She never remarried. Mrs. Miller knocked on their door last month when she was locked out of her house. She wanted to use the telephone to call her sister.

"It isn't Mrs. Miller," Barbara says.

"How do you know?" her husband asks.

"Because she hides a key on her porch now. She told me."

Barbara's husband nods. "Well then," he says, "I'll just look through the peephole. Will that make you happy?"

"Alan," Barbara says. But before she can say anything else, he's looking through the peephole. He glances back at Barbara then. His face is pale.

"What's wrong?" Barbara says.

"It's Mrs. Miller," Barbara's husband says in an uncharacteristically soft voice.

"What do you mean it's Mrs. Miller?"

"Mrs. Miller is standing out there, but—"

"But what?"

"There's something wrong with her," Barbara's husband says.

"What's wrong?"

"She's—well, she's bleeding,"

Barbara drops her book and stands from the chair. She moves toward the foyer, brushing past her husband. She begins to unfasten the door chain.

"Wait," her husband says.

Barbara turns to look at him. "Mrs. Miller is *bleeding*, Alan."

"She is," he says. "But it's not just that. It's—it's the way she's bleeding."

"What way?"

"All over," her husband says. "From everywhere at once. Eyes and nose and mouth and—"

"My God," Barbara says. She turns and looks through the peephole. But there's no one outside. The yellow circle of light on the porch is empty. Barbara hears her husband laughing. She's angry at first. But then she turns to look at him. And she realizes he's laughing like he used to when he was young, when they were at college together.

"Alan," she says. "That was awful."

"Your face," he says.

"You told me Mrs. Miller was bleeding all over," Barbara says. "How was my face supposed to look? The poor old woman."

Her husband is still laughing.

"What made you decide to do a thing like that?" Barbara asks.

He shakes his head. "I was washing the dishes. My hands were down in the warm water. And it just sort of occurred to me. It seemed like it would be funny."

Barbara shakes her head. "You're funny all right," she says. She thinks she might slap him like she used to. Not hard, of course, but in a playful way.

Then there's a knock at the door.

Barbara turns to look.

"What?" her husband says.

Barbara listens, wondering if it will happen again. "Didn't you hear it?" she says.

"Hear what?"

Barbara studies her husband. "Is this the second part of your prank?" she asks.

"Prank? Barbara—"

"Someone just knocked on the door, Alan," she says.

He looks surprised.

"How did you do it?" Barbara asks. "How did you make it sound like someone knocked?"

"I didn't do anything," her husband says. "I was standing here talking to you."

"Did you tap your foot?" Barbara says, looking down at her husband's shoe.

"I didn't even *hear* anything," he says.

Barbara turns toward the door. She puts her hand on the chain.

"Wait," her husband says.

"Why should I wait?" Barbara says.

"Because this doesn't seem right. I'm really sorry. I shouldn't have tried to trick you like that. It wasn't nice of me. And if you're playing a trick on me now, I deserve it."

Barbara thinks her husband looks sincere. He's a good actor though. He used to act in college. Once, she saw him in a play. He kissed her afterwards in the alley behind the theater. He still had his costume on, and Barbara felt like she was in the play too. She realizes now it's entirely possible her husband is not afraid at all.

Barbara turns and looks through the peephole. There's no one standing in the yellow circle of light on the porch. And there's no one in the shadows of the yard either.

Barbara makes a sound at the back of her throat.

"What?" her husband says.

Barbara shakes her head. She walks back to her chair in the living room. She sits down calmly and takes another sip of wine. Then she picks up her novel and starts to read.

"You're *reading*?" her husband says.

"I am," Barbara says.

"But you said you heard—"

"I know what I said," she replies. "Why don't you just go back and finish the dishes?"

Her husband doesn't move from the foyer.

Everything is silent.

Then Barbara hears her husband unfasten the door chain. She hears him turn the door handle. "Alan," she says. She realizes she wants to tell him to wait. But there's no time for that. He has already opened the door. He's walking outside onto the porch. "Alan?" she says again. He doesn't answer. Barbara stands and walks into the foyer. She looks out onto the porch. There's no one in the pool of yellow light. She looks into the darkened yard beyond. There's no one. She wants to call out, to tell her husband this isn't funny. When he used to pull pranks in college, they were always harmless things. But this—

Barbara pauses. She knows what she has to do. She steps back inside the house and closes the front door. Then she waits.

Finally, there's a knock.

Barbara goes to the peephole and looks out. Her husband is there. He's smiling.

"Alan?" Barbara says.

He doesn't respond.

When Mrs. Miller knocked on the door last month, it had been Barbara who went to answer. She peered out through the peephole and saw Mrs. Miller, small and shivering, in the pool of yellow light. Barbara had opened the door. Mrs. Miller told her that she'd gotten locked out of the house. It had been such a foolish thing. Barbara looked at Mrs. Miller and thought about what it would feel like to be so old and alone. She felt sorry for Mrs. Miller. But, more than that, she felt glad she herself was not old and alone. Barbara was thirty-seven. She had Alan. Cheerful Alan who always was kind and often thoughtful.

"I'm not going to open the door, Alan," Barbara says, standing in the foyer. "You can stay out there in the cold."

She looks through the peephole again.

Alan is in the same spot in the yellow pool of light, still smiling. He looks like he did when they were young. In fact, Barbara realizes, he looks *exactly* like he did when they were young. He doesn't look like her husband anymore. He looks like a photograph of the boy she met in astronomy class. The boy who would smile at her as if he knew a secret.

"Alan," she says through the closed door. "What are you doing? What's wrong?"

He doesn't answer. He only smiles.

Barbara thinks of Mrs. Miller then. She thinks of Mrs. Miller's husband who died in a car accident. Barbara never met him. He died before she and Alan moved into the neighborhood. She wonders what his name was. She wonders if she's ever heard Mrs. Miller speak the name out loud.

Barbara realizes her husband has now come closer to the door. He touches the door handle. He moves it back and forth.

Barbara thinks about something her husband once said to her in astronomy class. He said: "What if we get married, Barbara? What if we get married and live together like an old man and old woman?"

It was Barbara's turn to laugh then. She told him not to be silly.

"I don't know if it's silly," he said.

And then he made a face: mouth open, eyes wide.

Like he was surprised by something terrible.

Fantasy Kit/1942

A) Two American soldiers, midwestern boys with all their strength about them, eighteen and twenty-three. A dim-lit bar. Italy. The smell of chicory. Is it Christmas Eve? It is Christmas Eve. Snow falls beyond the darkened window.

1. One of the soldiers has "chestnut-colored hair." The other is blond (field of wheat/late autumn).
2. Both men smile frequently, nervously.

B) Pool of light. Soft light. Yellow music.

1. Dialogue: "...waiting for me back home..."
2. Dialogue: "...never quite the same though..."
3. Dialogue: "...I had a dog when I was boy. A big farm mutt..."
4. Dialogue: "...what would it be like?"

C) Nostalgia is a color. A filter for the light.

D) [Question: Do you find erotic possibilities in violence?]

E) One of the soldiers, in early years, walked with his

grandfather to a low stone bridge over a creek. The soldier stood with his grandfather (a farmer) on the bridge and watched small fish dart in the shadows of the water. The two did not speak. They watched the fish for nearly an hour. Then they returned to the grandfather's farmhouse and sat in the wooden chairs beneath the oak tree. This was a good memory that would remain with the soldier for the rest of his life.

F) An alley behind the Italian bar. Snow falls in the silent dark. Two soldiers. Midwestern boys with all their strength about them. Do they strip off their pressed uniforms? No. They do not strip off their pressed uniforms.

1. The dark-haired soldier kneels on the cold cobblestones before the blond soldier.
2. He unzips the young man's trousers.
3. The blond soldier does not look at the dark-haired soldier. Instead, he stares at an empty space in the distance.
4. He does not stare at an empty space in the distance because he is displeased.
5. He stares because that is what he has taught himself to do when he feels sexual excitement or fear.
6. As he stares at the empty space in the distance, a landscape appears that does not exist: country lake, water glittering in sunlight. Something rises from the lake, a pale figure, gray-headed.

G) The member/penis.

1. Veined like funeral marble.
2. Thickness.

3. A veiled head. Pink. The shape of an arrow.
4. Already, a clear fluid.

H) [Question: What does it mean to be drained of time?]

Alternate Kit: Death Kit.

1. *Both boys will be dead by the end of the war.*
2. *One boy will be dead by the end of the war.*
3. *Neither boy will be dead by the end of the war.*
4. *One of the soldiers—on a dark night when rain falls in gray sheets—will come to understand that dreams are the soul's memory of the body.*

I) Improvisational logic? Retrospective confabulation?

J) *I like to see you standing there so young. Younger than you think. I had almost forgotten.*

K) Two American soldiers, midwestern boys with all their strength about them. A country lake, water glittering in sunlight. Above the lake hangs a pale figure, a phantom. The figure is neither alive nor dead. The figure watches the soldiers kiss. They kiss on the mouth. The soldiers caress each other. They are in love in the way two men can be in love. The gray phantom does not move as it watches, does not shift its ragged sheets. The phantom does not want to betray its own existence.

Pan and Hook

Do not imagine me nymph, nor fey, nor ragged spirit of the air. I am a stranger body still, fine-limbed and silver-horned. Once, I walked on burnished hooves through the leafy shade of unspoiled Arcadia. Shadows of lush fir spilled over me. I carried a flute of tethered reeds. And there was always music or at least the memory of it. I tripped from stone to stone, sometimes pausing to pick lice from the fur of my hindquarters. My mind was quiet, stilled by trees and streams. But in my heart, there hung a kind of longing: a heavy, dripping nest. It was difficult to name all the creatures that inhabited the nest. I could only say I knew they would never leave me. And I, in turn, would never be permitted to take my leave of them.

How many a handsome soldier did I frighten on those long-ago forest paths? Men, in the dusky light, grew startled at the sound of my music. They claimed to glimpse a pair of lamp-lit eyes. They heard a violent rustling. There were stories told about me around the campfire. The Beast of Parnon stalks us, they said, the goat-god of the wilderness. And yet, I meant those Romans no harm. In truth, I longed to hold them, to comfort them in their fear. I wanted to kiss their full Roman lips and stroke the hard white scars on their shoulder blades.

I remember one dark-haired boy, a youth whose name I never learned. I chased him into a copse of alder trees. He trembled. Then he prayed.

"What have I done?" he said. "The gods—they are angry."

I attempted a gentle expression. “I am not angry,” I said.

The boy fell to his knees. He shook and wept. Later, I learned he drowned himself in the Tiber.

*

There was an earlier age, of course, more rustic and more faith-filled. I was worshiped then. Priests made sacrifices in my name. Pindar writes that the virgins sang of me. They called me Ba’al and Tammuz. They wailed and struck their breasts. In truth, the songs of virgins did not interest me. Instead of listening to their paeans, I would climb the barren hillsides. And in the cover of darkness, I’d teach handsome shepherds to touch themselves in nighttime fields. I instructed those men how to soothe one another too. How to kiss and be kind. I remember the scent of the herdsmen, flesh and sweat and leather. They lay together amongst the broken pillars of long-dead civilizations, wrapped in one another’s arms. They grew satisfied, clear of eye. And that, to me, was worship.

*

But there are no longer shepherds on the hill or Roman soldiers in the wood. Man is a fool for time. And always, he abandons his gods. Here is how I too was abandoned: One morning, a sailor called Thamus—not a particularly beautiful or interesting boy—was on his way to Florence. Near the coast, he heard what he believed to be a divine voice floating over the water. The voice, in haunted tones, said: *Pan is dead. Proclaim it. The Great God Pan is dead.* I was in the forest when I heard the echo of those words. I listened all day and into the evening, hoping for some refute. But the wood remained silent. And I knew the incantation that the voice had spoken was somehow true. The boy, Thamus, repeated it in village and city: *Pan is dead. Pan is dead.* The dreadful words, over and again. And Pan *was* dead. As was Ba’al and Tammuz and even the Beast of Parnon. I was left a nameless thing. Forsaken.

*

I retreated to an island then, a bleak outcropping in the sea. The rock was small enough to have no name. White lilies grew from crags, and great storms sometimes welled. I took no interest such things. I did not play my pipe or gambol along the shores. I hoped only that this place, this empty Never-Was, might be a vessel strong enough to hold my grief. I told myself I must learn to feel at home on the cold island. For I too would "never be" again. I found a grotto. I slept in a cave near a pool of black water. And there I did not dream. For what would be the point of dreaming?

And then one day, many years after my arrival on the island, I heard a clamor upon the sea. There was shouting and then canon fire. I scuttled from my cave and perched upon a stone to watch two great ships do battle in the island's narrow cove. I saw fire. The ocean itself turned dark with ash. And after a long while, when one ship had sunk and the other had sailed away victorious, I slunk back to my cave, wondering whom the dying men might have prayed to in their last moments.

It was then, on the rocky rim of my home, that I saw a smear of blood. The blood smelled human. It smelled male. My heart quickened. I peered into the darkness of my cave and discerned there a shape: a man, hunched and shivering. I realized he must have been one of the sailors from the sunken ship. He'd somehow dragged himself here from the sea. The man was handsome, dark, wearing a red coat with buttons made of gold. His black hair dripped with brine. The fingers of one hand trembled on his knee.

I crawled toward him in the darkness, hoping not to frighten him. The sailor, perhaps the captain of the sunken ship according to his regalia, bled. He'd been wounded in the battle. A deep cut ran across his cheek. And his left hand, I realized, was entirely missing. It had been hacked away. Yellow bone, hook-like in its shape, protruded from the meat of his wrist.

The sailor opened his eyes when he heard my approach. It had been so long since I was close to a man, since I'd smelled a man's scent and felt a man's breath. I realized, in that moment, how badly I wanted this sailor. If he would not worship me, at least he might know me, make me feel as though I continued to exist. To my amazement, he did not recoil at my approach. Instead, he smiled wanly. "Peter—" he whispered there in the darkness of the cave. His lips were bloodless, nearly white. "You're covered in dirt. You've been playing—the river."

I said nothing. For I was not, nor had I ever been, called "Peter." And I did not know what river he spoke of.

"I'm sorry," the sailor said. "I'm so sorry." He winced in pain. "I've wanted to tell you—so many years—I sailed—"

I leaned forward, imagining, for a brief moment, that this bleeding sailor in his red jacket might be the ghost of the other sailor, Thamus, who had long ago proclaimed my death. Thamus had finally come to apologize to me.

Then the sailor spoke again: "You called me *James*," he said. "You tried to hold my hand there by the river. To kiss me. I said you were mad, a strange little nymph. The river Eton, the place we used to go—remember how bright the sun was on those afternoons, Peter?"

I looked into the sailor's eyes.

He did not see me, but instead appeared to recall some long-ago moment.

"I pretend from time to time—" he said. "I pretend that—" He reached for me. "Come closer, Peter."

I crouched.

"Will you stroke my cheek," he said, "as you used to do?"

I touched him, ever so gently, with the sharp claw of my hand.

He raised and lowered his own bleeding stump. It appeared as though he thought he was stroking me as well.

"The ship came upon us swiftly," he whispered. "Pirates. Just off the coast of the island. What is the name of this island, Peter?"

Never-Was, I thought.

He sighed. "And my hand—my poor hand."

I gazed at the yellow shard of bone emerging from his wrist.

The sailor spread his lips, showing blood on his teeth. "So strange—" he said. "I dreamed of you just last night, Peter. We were together on board the ship, the Roger. Only, in my dream, it did not sail upon the waters. It *flew*. We travelled together through the clouds. I held you, and we watched a flock of gulls move around us like a school of silvery porpoises. When night fell, we did not land but glided still amongst the bright lamps of the stars."

I touched the sailor's cheek again. His flesh had turned cold.

"I wish you would kiss me now," James said. "As once you wished to do."

I leaned forward. But before my lips touched his, I paused. Why I did, I cannot say. For wasn't this what I'd longed for? Wasn't this what I'd most desired? Yet to have it now, with a dying man—

It was in that pause that the sailor's eyelids fluttered. His gaze seemed to focus. And his expression changed. Fear passed over his dark features. He saw me for what I was. Not Peter, but the Goat. Not the boy he once loved. But something he could not even imagine. Something that lived hidden away on an island. Something awful and sad.

The sailor's phantom hand fell away. His breath grew still.

Somewhere in the distance, I heard the divine voice speaking once again. *Pan is dead. And Peter is dead. And now so too, the captain.*

I lay down next to the dead man and put my arms around him.

We remained like that as the sun set on the island and the night birds began to sing.

A Roman Road

They come from Rome, the revelers, all gold and violet tattered. They come in carts and broken litters, sedans and palanquins. They ride on bridled mules and once-fine horses. They walk and limp and drink a bitter wine. They remember (however vaguely) a prior age, a higher light: plumed gardens full of olive trees, a villa strung with burning lamps. They remember halls of fine marble, the lips of pale young men. They sing and show their teeth and move their strange procession along the dusty road. Some wear masks of ivory, some of hammered silver, others still are bare-faced. One of them, a tall man with long arms, carries a horn. He uses it to make a reedy sound. Another strums a broken harp. And still another pounds a clay urn as if it were a drum. The sky is vague and white. The trees, dead and leafless. The revelers do not pause to look at the ruins on the outskirts of their city. They know the ruins well enough. Fallen aqueducts and shattered tombs, rose-colored brickwork, all in pieces. Here in the countryside, the hills are brown and burned. And the autumn wind seems to bear a message: *take comfort, men, for all is dying, all will soon be dead.* But these revelers, they do not pause, they do not listen. They make their way deeper into the country, moving toward the valley of the Tiber. They know their destination well enough: the storied pleasure dome, the labyrinth and the feasting hall. The country house where Roman men have always come when they are in need of delight. These revelers remember their fathers traveling to such a place. They've heard stories all their lives. And now they too want to drink the house's wine and eat its fabled dish, the stewed tongues of songbirds. They want to lay in dark chambers and stroke the house's handsome ghosts (the limber soldiers and the athletes and the dark-eyed youths who once lounged on the steps of the Forum). These men, the last of the revelers, they want this country palace, this dream. The Huns and Vandals will not harm them there. Falling will not harm them. They remember, as they walk together, what their fathers called this place: "My house of gray forgetting. My spilling forth. My dust."

A Horror

I'm thinking of a movie.

I can't remember the title.

I saw it in a theater in Brixton.

One of the old dark theaters down there.

The ceiling was painted to look like a starry sky.

I didn't recognize any of the constellations.

Trees were painted on the walls: myrtle and boxwood, cypress and oleander.

The movie was about a group of young people.

One of them was so handsome.

He wore his hair long like they used to. He was the leader of the group.

I remember I liked his voice. I liked listening to him.

Tom, I think he was called. Or Tod.

I'll call him Tom.

I remember that the young people made their way together through a forest.

Tom told them he had some destination in mind.

The whole group followed because they liked Tom so much. They admired him.

The destination was somewhere Tom had visited as a child.

A cave or a lake.

Let's just say it was a lake.

Tom talked about the lake as they walked.

He talked about an event he remembered from his childhood.

The group asked questions.

Tom said he couldn't answer the questions. The lake, he said, pulled memories down. It hid them all away.

One of the other members of the group was called Bill.

Bill had short black hair and wore a black t-shirt even though the sun was shining.

Bill was in love with Tom.

It wasn't a crush.

It was love.

Bill had felt this way about Tom since they were boys.

He'd always imagined what it would feel like to kiss Tom on the mouth. What Tom would taste like.

I should add I'm not sure how Tom himself felt about Bill.

Tom had a certain way of looking at everyone in the group.

Not with love exactly.

But he had these large eyes, expressive.

They were some wonderful color.

Tom would run his fingers through his long hair and gaze thoughtfully at his group of friends.

They all gazed back at him.

His beauty seemed to form a circle of protection.

That's what they thought at least.

There were other characters in the movie besides Tom and Bill.

I don't remember most of them.

But there was at least one other character who seemed important.

Her name was Jane.

Jane was smart.

If anyone had a question—something Tom couldn't answer—they asked Jane.

And Jane always knew the answer.

I remember, early in the film, Jane tripped on a branch in the forest.

There was a loud sound, a sort of snap.

Jane said something had happened to her ankle.

Everyone gathered around Jane. Tom examined the ankle carefully. He said it might be broken. Jane said it wasn't. Tom asked if she wanted to go back to the car. They'd all come together to the woods in an old brown car. Jane said no. She could walk if someone would help her. It was Bill who offered to help. Bill was like that, always kind. As long as the kindness didn't take him too far away from Tom.

So Jane leaned on Bill and hobbled along.

They all made their way toward the lake.

Tom told a story.

It was an old story.

Something he'd read in a book.

The story was about a group of young people who went out into the wilderness to see something.

They didn't come back. Not in the way people usually come back.

The story went on for a long while.

Bill got lost in the story. He forgot how much he loved Tom.

And Jane forgot about the pain in her ankle.

I suppose I shouldn't dwell too long on this walk through the forest.

But in my mind, the walk and the story Tom told took up most of the film.

Eventually, the group arrived at the lake, or what I'm now remembering as a lake. It might have been a cave, as I said, or even a stream. But likely it was a lake. A big dark lake in the middle of the woods.

Jane sat down on a log because her ankle hurt so much.

I remember the actress who played Jane was very good at portraying suffering.

She could do it without even moving her face.

I remember Tom asked Jane if she would be all right there on the log while the rest of them went to explore the lake.

Jane said she would be fine. She spoke firmly. She always spoke firmly to Tom, as if he was a child.

Tom nodded. Then he looked at Bill.

This was the moment in the film where I believed Tom might actually be in love with Bill, just as Bill was in love with Tom.

The look that passed between them, it meant something.

I wondered if Tom and Bill might kiss before the movie was over. I hoped for it. I wanted to see that.

The group, five young people in all, moved toward the lake.

When they arrived at the dark edge of the water, they all began to realize, one by one, it wasn't a lake at all.

They'd been mistaken.

It was, instead, a tall figure, standing in a grove.

The figure, draped in gray robes, was as tall as the tallest of the trees.

Its skin was the color of marble.

The figure did not look at the young people.

Instead, it stared into the far distance as if remembering something.

Bill spoke first. He didn't speak loudly. He said, "Tom, what is this?"

Tom didn't answer. He seemed to be remembering something too.

And then, at that moment, the giant figure standing in the grove began to lower its massive head to look down at the youths in the field.

From Jane's perspective, it looked as though all of her friends had waded waist-deep into the lake.

They seemed like they might go deeper still. And this worried Jane. Her friends were fully clothed. Their clothes would fill with water and grow heavy.

Jane stood. Her ankle hurt.

"Tom?" she called.

But Tom didn't turn to look at her.

Bill didn't turn.

I remember I didn't look back at her either.

Jane began to limp toward the lake.

"Don't go any deeper," she called.

But we'd all gone deeper already.

We were up to our chins in the water.

And the tall gray figure spoke to us then.

It said: *How vain are these thousand years?*

It said: *I remember when the trees were white and full with blossom.*

And the water of the lake grew deeper still.

And I knew then that Tom would never kiss Bill.

And poor Jane would never reach us.

The gray figure would continue to speak, going on and on.

And we would all wonder how we'd gotten ourselves here, so many years in the past, so many years, in such a strange and flickering light.

A Memory of the Christ by the Apostle John

And the Word was made flesh, and it dwelt among us. I remember how that flesh felt against mine, thin and made of bones. Ribs pressed to skin. Arms, long and frail. He was like a gentle animal, left too long at pasture. I remember thinking to myself, this is not the body of the Christ. This is the body of a man. Good but not strong. I could feel His breath against my neck. I could smell the oil of His hair. Our room was hot, even after the sun had set. A gentle wind moved the branches of the olive tree that grew in the garden beyond. He would whisper to me in the darkness as we lay upon our pallet. He said: "John, I will tell you things I cannot tell the others." And He held me in His arms, as John the Baptist once held Him in the river. There were times, I think, He believed I *was* that other John. He confessed to me He had strange dreams. He said He walked in the places between the stars. And the darkness there felt like a lonely house. In these dreams, He wished He was not alone. He wished I was there with Him. I said I could not walk with Him in the places between the stars. I was not like Him. And He would kiss my neck with the same mouth that He used to speak to the people. He would say, "John, we are not so different." And He believed that was true. I remember I closed my eyes. I felt Him press against me as His kisses grew more passionate. And when He was finally inside of me for the first time, something happened I knew I could never tell Him. When He was inside of me, I was no longer with Him on the pallet in our room. Instead, I walked in the places between the stars. I walked for a long while. And the darkness there did not feel like a lonely house to me. No, the darkness was crowded with forms, the shapes of men and women, suspended just beyond the edges of my vision. Their mouths hung open. Their eyes were wide. And it was then that I saw what they saw: the absence of light was not an empty thing. Every space here, every particle, was inhabited. And it was a cold figure who lived in that space. A figure who would never speak, who would never give Word. Something had been mistaken. Something misunderstood. I remember I called out on the pallet in our small hot room. And the Christ, good man, thrust deeper, believing I called out in ecstasy.

Plumed and Armored, We Came

Calcutta, 1859

Father took me to the hot country. The air was full of flies. Rows of poppies grew in fields like faces in a portrait gallery. I walked with Father along a sunbaked road. He was dressed in a suit of white linen. He looked, to me, like some bright spirit or a figure of the upper air. Mother and Thomas had been dead for almost a year. I missed them every day. Father missed them too. He did not tell me so, but I knew his feelings well enough.

As we walked, I remembered Mother's face on the morning of her death. She lay in her bed: eyes open, mouth open. She had a startled look. She held little Thomas in her arms. His eyes, the lids of which had the most delicate of blond lashes, were closed. I'd wanted to touch the lashes one last time. But Father would not allow me to do so. He said I must let Thomas rest.

A tall servant with an umbrella followed Father and me along the hot road. The servant attempted to provide shade. When he lagged, Father spoke to him unkindly. "I cannot see the fields in all this dreadful light," Father said. "And if I cannot see the fields—if I cannot count the poppies—do you know what will happen then?"

The tall servant did not reply. Perhaps, he spoke no English. Or perhaps he did not know the answer to Father's question.

I knew the answer well enough. If Father did not correctly assess the fields, his employers at the East India Company would be upset with him. Mr. Watts and Mr. Brandt would send Father a letter. Father would read it and grow angry. He would toss the letter into the fire. This had happened once before, shortly after the death of Mother and Thomas.

In the heat of the afternoon, milk leaked from the poppy flowers. It seemed to me the flowers were crying. I asked Father the reason for this.

He looked up from the leather journal where he made his notes and said: "It's because they recognize us, Victoria."

"The flowers recognize us?" I said.

He nodded absently. "They see through time," he said. "They know the splendor of the Empire. 'Plumed and armored, we came. Plumed and armored—'"

I did not understand his meaning. But this was not unusual. Father often quoted from old poems he'd memorized at school. Mother used to laugh cheerfully at his pretenses. She'd attempt to pull at his mustache. Then Father would laugh too.

That evening, Father went to his study to write a letter to Mr. Watts and Mr. Brandt. I lay down and closed my eyes in my hot little bedroom. Soon, I fell into a state of fitful dreaming. In my dream, I wandered in the shadow of a golden cliff. Near the base of the cliff, I found a city made of bronze and stone. I walked the empty streets of the city until I came to a large, pillared house. It was clearly the home of a gentleman. I knocked on the door. I felt a strong urge to tell the owner of this house I was lost. I wanted to ask for his help. But when the door opened, there was no gentleman to greet me. Instead, I saw what I, at first, took to be a large poppy flower. The flower grew in the shadows of the foyer, meaty green stalk rising from a crack in the marble floor. Its thick-veined leaves were as large as human hands. And it had silky red petals and rings of black stamen. A yellow pistil extended from its center. I stepped into the foyer of the house. The closer I drew to the flower, the more I began to believe this was no flower at all. It was far too large. It towered over me. And it made a soft humming sound, as if it sang quietly to itself. I came to stand beneath its leaves. Then the flower shifted, lowering its silky head to look down at me. It had blue eyes. Blue like mother's eyes. And its mouth hung open like mother's mouth when she was dead.

When I awoke, I was crying. I found I could not stop crying.

Father came to the doorway of my bedroom and peered in at me. His dark hair was disheveled. His eyes, red-rimmed. He held the tincture bottle, the "health remedy," made from the milk of the poppy flowers. He had given the health remedy to Mother before she died. She had a nervous cough. Mother, in turn, gave the health remedy to Thomas for his crying.

"Are you unwell, Victoria?" Father asked.

"I am," I said, putting my face in my hands. "I am unwell." And it was true. The tears would not stop falling.

Father came to sit on the edge of my bed. "You must take some of this," he said, indicating the small brown bottle. "But we must not give you too much, Victoria."

"Not as much as Mother took," I said.

Father nodded.

"And not as much as Thomas took either."

He nodded again.

"Be careful when you put it on the spoon," I said.

"I will be careful," he replied.

Father produced the spoon from the pocket of his suit coat. He poured out a small amount of dark liquid. I knew it would taste good, like sweet treacle.

The next day, Father and I attended a party in a grand garden. Father said the garden belonged to a prince. Many poppies grew in the prince's garden. Their red petals looked so fine in the bright afternoon sun. White peacocks roamed the stony paths. Father ventured off to speak to another Englishman, someone he said he recognized. While he was gone, an old woman came to stand beside me. She wore a yellow scarf. I imagined she might be the mother of the prince. She showed me a set of tattered embroideries. At first, I did not understand what was depicted in their beadwork. Greenish bodies stood upright in what appeared to be open stone graves. Several of the figures were men. There was a woman too. And there was even a little child wrapped tightly in a winding-sheet. All of the figures were corpses, and all were awake, wide-eyed. The woman in the yellow scarf touched the jewels in her embroidery. I recognized some of the jewels: pearl and moonstone, topaz and carbuncle.

"What is its meaning?" I said. "Please—"

The woman continued to stroke the jewels.

Father appeared beside us then, brow furrowed. "What's this?" he asked the old woman, gesturing at the embroidery.

She looked at him. She did not appear startled or afraid.

"Why would you invite a child to look at such things?" Father said.

The woman folded the fabric carefully. She walked away, leaving us alone.

"Was that not the mother of the prince?" I asked Father.

"It was not," he said. "Most certainly, it was not."

He took my hand and said he had learned we were to be introduced to the prince's chief advisor. This was an important meeting, according to Father. He and the advisor were to discuss the status of the fields. "Such introductions, they rattle me," he said. "Nerves—not good at all, Victoria." He took the health remedy from the pocket of his suit, unscrewed the cap and put the bottle to his lips.

I watched him drink. After he was done, I reached up, fingers splayed.

Father started to take the spoon from his jacket, but I shook my head. He put the bottle in my hand. "Careful now," he said. "Not too much."

I lifted the dark bottle to my own lips and thought of my dream. I thought of how cruel dreams could be. I drank some of the health remedy and thought of the old woman's tapestries. I drank more. The sweet tincture was so delicious in the summer heat.

Father's eyes had turned dark and glassy. He squeezed my hand as we walked. "'Off they went, those fine and flowered guards,'" he whispered keenly, "'across an emerald plane.'" We moved together toward a stone house where the prince's advisor waited. "We will show these men, Victoria," Father said. "We will show them how fine—"

I slowed then. My face felt hot. And my chest was suddenly too warm. I tugged at Father's hand. He paused. I stumbled.

Father tried to catch me, but I slipped through his grasp.

A peacock opened its fan of white feathers. As I lay in the grass of the garden, I found I could not cause myself to breathe.

And all around us, red poppies turned their heads to look.

Deep in the Hundred Acre Wood

Do we not go to the forest at midnight?

Do we not sit in the brambled dark at the fine table there?

Is the table not made of a large tree stump, draped in a linen cloth?

Have the owl and the field mouse not set the table with silver trenchers and colored glass?

Do we not have before us polished spoons and mirrors and salt cellars shaped like shells from the sea?

Do we not eat sweet honey cakes from gilded plates and drink black tea from Chinese cups?

Do our tails not curl and our ears not tremble?

Do we not speak in the manner we have spoken for a thousand years?

Do we not talk of the hollows and the cave on the hill and the old magic that is buried in the tangled roots of the great oak tree?

Does the frog not stand and do his silly dance?

Does the pig not make complaints to the donkey?

And on the longest night of the year, as the dead leaves fall and we drink our strongest tea, does a boy not come out of the bracken and into our midst? Is he not a frail-looking boy dressed in a yellow shirt and short pants? And does the boy not tell us he is lost? Does he not say he has been walking all day and night in the forest?

Do we not, as we listen, chew our honey cakes with sharp beaks and pointed teeth?

Do our whiskered muzzles not twitch?

And does the boy not tell us his name and ask that we should help him, that we should return him to his father who lives in the big stone house at the edge of the forest?

And do we not remember when this boy's father used to run with his own brothers in years past and hunt us and make us fall into traps?

Do we not remember the pain of that?

Does the rabbit not don his wire rimmed spectacles to examine the dirty-faced boy?

Does the rabbit not wiggle his nose and twitch his ears?

And after he has made his examinations, do we not invite the boy to sit with us at our table?

Is the boy not still crying?

Does he not wipe muddied tears from his cheeks and ask again to be returned to his father?

And do we not gaze at him, eyes shining like new moonlight, as we imagine the cave near the great oak tree?

Is there not a creature who lives there in that cave, a black thing that does not speak and looks something very much like a bear?

(Though, surely, it is not a bear.)

(For the man in the stone house killed the bear many years ago.)

(He took the bear's bloodied hide.)

(We buried what was left of our friend beneath the great oak tree.)

And do we not picture what will happen when we've finished our tea and we lead the boy past the tree to the mouth of the cave on the hill?

Will the boy not ask: "Who lives here in this dark cave"?

And will we not reply: "Someone who was always hungry, child. Someone who is hungry still"?

The Maze

Rome 438 C.E.

1.

Ruined edge of a ruined city.

2.

Here the fallen aqueducts, the shattered tombs. Rose-colored brickwork all silvered over with lichen.

3.

Horatius is aware of his crime. He offended the senator, Gnaeus Sabinus. Horatius would not be penetrated in the alley behind the Temple of Saturn. The senator grew angry and called the guards.

4.

Horatius is taken in a wooden cart to the place of punishment. The place of punishment has no name. The gates are covered in valerian, a gray weed. Two figures greet him. They are taller than most men and wear masks made to look like the faces of animals. One man is a tiger. The other, a lynx.

5.

Horatius wants to run toward the river. He could jump into the water, swim downstream toward the black mountains. But the masked figures have already opened the gates. They take him by the arms and drag him into a courtyard.

6.

"Please," Horatius says. But the men do not relent. They push him down a steep staircase. He lands on his hands and knees. He is cut, bleeding. Horatius looks back up the stairs. The tall figures close the iron gate. They lock it. When Horatius does not move, the lynx-man says: "There is a door on the other side of the maze. If you make it to the door, you are free."

7.

Horatius lifts a burning torch from its sconce. The tiger-man and the lynx-man talk quietly behind the gate at the top of the stairs. Horatius moves slowly down the narrow stone passage. He worries the corridor will grow narrower still. Soon he will be forced to turn sideways in order to walk.

8.

Horatius thinks of his mother. She does not know he has been taken away. She does not know he spends time with the men in the alley behind the Temple of Saturn. She will wonder where he has gone. She will weep for him.

9.

Horatius comes to a fork in the path. He searches for some stone or pebble to mark the path he chooses. But there is no stone or pebble. The maze is swept clean. Horatius wonders who sweeps the maze. Is it the tiger-man and the lynx-man? He realizes the palms of his hands are still bleeding. He presses the palm of his right hand to the wall of the right-branching path. Then he moves down the path. The halls here are all the same. But Horatius makes them different, marking each choice with blood.

10.

Soon, Horatius comes to a corridor that is already marked. There is a handprint. Yet, when he holds his torch close to the handprint, the blood does not glisten. It is old blood, dried. Someone else had the same idea as Horatius. He wonders then if that other person was able to escape the maze.

As if summoned, there is a sound ahead of him, the scrape of a sandal against stone. Horatius grows still. It is likely a monster who lives in the maze. The monster has smelled his blood and come to devour him. Horatius does not run. Instead, he extends his torch into the darkness.

11.

A figure appears, half-obscured by shadow. The figure does not look like a monster.

"Hello?" Horatius says.

The figure raises a hand in greeting.

"How did you come to be here?" Horatius asks.

There is a pause. Then, the sound of a young man's voice: "The same way everyone comes to be here, I suppose."

"How long has it been?" Horatius says.

"There is no light in the catacomb," the figure says. "There are no days."

"Is there food?" Horatius asks. "Water?"

"There is food," the figure says. "And water."

"Where?" Horatius says.

The figure steps out of the shadows. He carries no torch. He wears a kind of cape and a mask made of hammered bronze. The mask does not look like an animal's face. Rather it resembles the face of a human. "You haven't travelled far enough," the young man says.

"Is there a way out?" Horatius says.

"Follow me," the young man replies.

12.

As they walk, the young man tells Horatius his story. It sounds much like Horatius's own. Someone wanted favors. The young man would not provide them. He was sent here, to the place of punishment with the gray walls.

13.

They walk for a long time. Horatius studies the walls. There are no new handprints, only old handprints. "You made these?" Horatius says, gesturing toward one dried print.

The young man nods.

"You've made many," Horatius says.

14.

They come then to a hall that is not like the other halls. It is a large room full of statuary. The statues are like those in the sacred places of Rome, painted faces, watching.

"Who are they?" Horatius asks.

"I don't know," the young man says. "Memories, maybe."

"Whose memories?"

The young man shakes his head. "I've spent a long time looking at them."

15.

Deeper still. Horatius and the young man come to a kind of subterranean amphitheater. There are rows of benches surrounding a circular stage. Vestiges of a tragedy remain. Walls have been painted to look as though they are covered in gray valerian weed. Open iron gates stand near the back of the stage. They look much like the gates of the place of punishment.

"The gates are the same as the ones I passed through when I arrived," Horatius says.

"That's what I thought too," the young man says.

"Was there a performance?"

"Once," the young man says. "But it didn't make a great deal of sense. Actors went about their daily lives, looking into the fountain, doing laundry in a basin. If anyone spoke, they did not speak loudly enough for the audience to hear."

"So there was an audience?" Horatius asks. "People came into the maze?"

The young man nods, bronze mask glinting in the torchlight.

16.

Horatius wants to ask the young man to remove his mask. Yet, at the same time, he does not feel it would be right to make such a request. If the young man wears a mask, he must wear it for some reason.

17.

Horatius and the young man walk down the aisle of the amphitheater to the stage. They step through the iron gate and pass onto a dirt road. There is a nighttime sky painted above.

"Look," the young man says.

Horatius looks. He sees a river. The black Tiber. It too is painted. There is a moon, and there are mountains.

18.

They rest there on the stage by the iron gate. Horatius worries that if he falls asleep, the young man in the bronze mask will leave him. He will run away into the maze. Horatius will be alone again.

19.

Sleep comes. When Horatius awakes, the masked young man is still there, sitting beside the iron gate, watching him. Horatius thinks the young man's gray eyes look kind. He wishes the young man would hold him. Sometimes the men behind the Temple of Saturn held him.

"We should keep moving," the young man says.

"Because we're trying to find the way out?" Horatius asks.

The young man says nothing.

They stand and make their way from the theater.

In the maze again, they follow dried handprints made of blood. Horatius wonders why they always choose paths already marked with handprints. He asks the young man.

"Because I am showing you what you need to see," the young man says.

"But we want to escape, don't we?" Horatius said. "The jailers, or whatever it is they are, said there is an exit on the other side of the maze."

"That is my understanding as well," the young man says. "But there are other places too." He pauses, then says: "Now I have a question for you."

"What is it?" Horatius says.

"You won't leave me, will you?" the young man asks. "You won't run away?"

Horatius blushes. "No," he says. "I won't run away."

The young man nods. "I was down here alone for so long."

20.

They come to a vast empty dining hall. There are tables and benches for a hundred men. Horatius feels oddly frightened when he sees the dining hall. He wonders why a place like this has been abandoned. “Did men once live here?” he asks.

“No,” the young man says. “I don’t think so.”

Horatius considers his masked companion once more. He wonders, for a moment, if the young man might be some kind of spirit, a shadow left down here in the darkness. He wonders if he himself is becoming a spirit too.

21.

At the back of the dining hall, they pause before the threshold of a darkened room.

“What is this place?” Horatius asks.

The young man takes Horatius’s torch. “Follow me,” he says. “It’s one of the things I want to show you.”

Horatius follows the young man into the darkened room.

The walls, all the way to the ceiling, are lined with masks.

Horatius stares at them.

There are masks of every sort, animal and human, demon and god. The masks are made of bronze and gold and wood.

“What are all these masks for?” Horatius asks.

“They’re not masks,” the young man says.

“What then?” Horatius says.

“Faces,” the young man replies.

Horatius feels cold.

The young man unfastens the leather straps that hold the bronze mask to his face.

22.

Beneath the bronze mask is another mask. This one is thin, made of silver. It looks something like Horatius's own face. The young man unfastens the silver mask as well.

23.

Beneath the silver mask is a city that looks much like Rome. Seven hills. Streets like canyons. All lit red by an evening sun.

24.

Beneath the city is Horatius's mother. She watches the street from the window of their rooms, wondering when her son will return home.

25.

Beneath Horatius's mother are the black mountains and a black river.

26.

Beneath the river is a wind that blows.

27.

The only thing that is not beneath any of these masks is what should be there: eyes, a mouth, the semblance of a face.

28.

Horatius turns to flee.

"You told me you wouldn't leave," the space behind the mask says. It speaks still in a young man's voice. It has a young man's yearning.

Horatius pauses. He turns back to the figure and looks into the empty hole where a face should be. "You aren't what I expected," he says.

"No," the emptiness replies.

Horatius finds he no longer feels quite so cold. "Have you been to the alley behind the House of Saturn?" he asks.

"I haven't," the emptiness says. "Will you tell me about it?"

Horatius nods. "I will."

"That's good," the emptiness says.

Horatius realizes how cruel it was of him to turn away.

"Do you want to choose one of these faces before we go?" the emptiness says, gesturing toward the masks that line the walls.

Horatius gazes up at the masks. They stare back at him. "No," he says finally. "I don't think we'll need any of those." He holds out his hand to the emptiness. "Come on. I'll tell my stories as we walk."

The Pool Party

Ohio, 1993

Kristin is late to Michael Amberson's pool party.

She's late because her mother has a migraine.

Kristin's mother gets dizzy and sees auras when she has migraines.

"What do the auras look like?" Kristin asked once.

"Green," her mother said.

Kristin sits with her best friend, Allie, at the edge of the crowded pool.

They move their feet in the water and watch Michael Amberson laugh at another boy's joke over near the pool house.

"Michael's cute," Allie says.

Kristin doesn't reply.

"You don't think he's cute?"

"I'm not sure," Kristin says.

"You act so weird lately," Allie says.

Kristin pauses. "Who's that?" She points toward the other side of the pool.

There's a boy standing at the fence line.

He faces the fence, as if he's studying something in the grain of the wood.

He isn't wearing a swimsuit like the rest of the people at the party. Instead, he wears an oversized white sweatshirt, a white baseball cap, and a pair of dark jeans.

"What do you mean?" Allie asks.

"That boy," Kristin says. "Who is it?"

Allie squints. "Who cares?"

"You know who it looks like?" Kristin says.

"Who?"

"Josh."

"What do you mean Josh?"

"I mean it looks like Josh Dalton." Kristin says.

Allie looks down at her feet in the water. Finally, she says, "Kristin, you really shouldn't—"

"Look at his hair," Kristin says.

There's a ruff of blond, nearly-white hair curling up from the back of boy's baseball cap.

"Just stop," Allie says.

Josh Dalton died in a car accident the previous summer.

He was driving home from a pool party.

The party was at Mark Loughlin's house, and Mark lived all the way out in the country.

Josh ran his car off the road and hit a tree.

There were pictures of the mangled red car in the newspaper the next day alongside Josh's school picture.

Everyone had liked Josh Dalton.

He was nice and made jokes that were actually funny.

After the accident, the halls of the school were quiet for almost a month.

Nobody talked in the lunchroom.

Nobody answered questions in class.

Eventually, the teachers stopped asking questions.

"If it isn't Josh," Kristin says, moving her foot in the warm water of the pool, "who is it?"

"I don't know," Allie says. "Maybe somebody's friend."

"Well, why's he looking at the fence like that?"

"Drugs," Allie says.

Suddenly, Michael Amberson is kneeling behind the two girls. He's shirtless, dripping wet. "You guys okay?" he says.

"We're fine," Kristin says. "But who's that over there?"

Michael Amberson looks across the pool to the place Kristin is pointing. He shakes his head. "I don't know. Paul?"

"It's not Paul," Kristin says. "Paul's standing over there." She gestures toward a tall blond boy near the grill.

"Kristin thinks it's Josh Dalton," Allie says.

"What?" Michael says. He sounds angry. "Why would you say a thing like that?"

"I didn't say it," Allie replies. "Kristin did."

"Well don't—I don't know—don't joke around like that," Michael says. "It's just a guy. Somebody probably invited him."

Michael stands and starts to walk away.

"I'm sorry," Kristin calls after him.

But Michael Amberson doesn't look back.

Kristin taps her foot against Allie's leg. "Hey, you shouldn't have said that."

"No," Allie replies. "I guess not."

"I'm going to go see who that boy is," Kristin says.

"Don't."

"Why?"

"Because what if it's—"

Someone splashes water near them.

Allie wipes chlorine from her eyes.

Kristin stands. "You can come with me if you want."

Allie crosses her arms. "I'll wait."

Kristin walks around the edge pool.

On the way, she passes Jill Fredrick.

Jill dated Josh Dalton for a while when they were sophomores, and Kristin wonders if she should ask Jill who she thinks the boy in the white sweatshirt is.

But, at the last moment, she decides against it.

Jill is a nice person.

A question like that might upset her. Just like Michael Amberson got upset.

Instead, Kristin focuses her attention on the boy again.

He's still staring at the fence.

His face is very near the fencepost.

So close, in fact, that his nose must be almost pressed against the grain.

Kristin remembers Molly Tanzer talking about how hard Josh Dalton hit his face in the accident. "He hit the steering wheel or something," Molly said. "I guess it pushed his face—I don't know how to say it—sort of backward."

"What do you mean backward?" Kristin said.

"Not backward, I guess. It pushed his face *in*. Like inside his head."

"How does anyone know something like that?" Kristin said.

"Tim McGreve's brother is a highway patrolman," Molly said.

Kristin didn't want to think about Josh's face like that.

She hadn't known him very well—the friendliest they ever got was that Josh sometimes said hi to her in the halls at school—but she still didn't want to think about him like that.

There was one time, after a football game in the fall, when Kristin saw Josh Dalton talking to a boy from another school.

The boy had thick black hair and dark eyebrows.

Josh and the dark-haired boy stood together under an oak tree near the back of the stadium.

Both of them had their hands stuffed into the pockets of their jackets. Like they were keeping them safe.

Their faces were pale.

Not in an unhealthy way, Kristin thought, but in an excited way.

She'd seen other boys get pale like that.

She heard Josh Dalton and the other boy laughing together.

She wondered if Josh had made a joke.

And then, when he probably thought no one was looking, Josh Dalton leaned forward and kissed the dark-haired boy on the mouth.

It wasn't a long kiss.

But it was long enough for the dark-haired boy to reach around and stroke Josh Dalton's back. He stroked Josh's back in an awkward way, like maybe he'd never done anything like that before, trailing his fingers along Josh's spine.

Kristin looked away then.

She knew she wasn't supposed to see the kiss or the way the dark-haired boy stroked Josh's back.

And yet she did see.

As Kristin walks toward boy in the white sweatshirt, he moves ever so slightly, shifting his weight from his left foot to the right.

Kristin wonders if the boy is finally going to turn around.

But he doesn't turn around.

He just stands there with his face against the fence.

Kristin is on his side of the pool now.

As she gets closer, she notices there's something odd about the boy's white sweatshirt.

At first, she thinks there's some kind of stain on it.

A long stain running all the way down the boy's back.

But the closer she gets, the more she thinks it isn't actually a stain.

It's more like a shadow.

Only there isn't anything near the boy that would cast a shadow.

There's no tree or pole or anything.

The boy shifts again, this time placing his weight back on his left foot.

It's as if he's rocking back and forth in slow motion.

"Hey," Kristin calls.

She's close enough now to talk to him.

But the boy doesn't respond.

The shadow appears to grow darker somehow, blacker on the white of the sweatshirt.

Kristin finally stands just behind the boy.

She reaches out to tap him on his shoulder.

Then she hears Allie say, "Kristin!" from somewhere behind her.

Kristin turns away from the boy.

She sees Allie standing maybe ten feet away.

Allie looks flushed, scared.

She's staring at something just behind Kristin.

Kristin feels dizzy.

She doesn't know why she feels dizzy, but she thinks it must be how her mom feels when she gets her migraines.

Kristin hears something move behind her.

Or maybe she doesn't hear it.

Because maybe it isn't a sound.

For a moment, Kristin thinks she can feel the shadow on the boy's white sweatshirt.

The shadow is like an arm.

She can feel it move up and down.

And now the shadow is less like an arm and more like a hole.

A deep black hole.

Kristin stares into it.

She stares into it so long that the darkness begins to look like light.

Someone is screaming there in the light.

Or maybe a lot of people are screaming.

Maybe everyone at the pool party is screaming now.

And Kristin is screaming too.

Loup-Garou

1.

Language is a closed system that bears no relationship to reality.

2.

I write about a prince. But I do not mean a prince. Instead, I mean a figure rendered.

3.

I render this particular figure (out of all possible figures) because I saw a play in Los Angeles last night in which actors pretended to be princes. The concept of a prince remains in my mind, a portrait in a gallery.

4.

I am from Ohio. My father is a farmer. I will never meet a prince. But I can, of course, render a prince.

5.

The mind is a closed system that bears no relationship to reality.

6.

I render a prince. He becomes *my* prince.

7.

Therefore [the prince comes down from the castle].

8.

I have seen castles in Europe. But I do not imagine those castles here. Nor do I imagine the castles I have seen in films. I do not imagine a castle at all, in fact. The castle remains an ambiguous object.

9.

Then [the prince wanders in the forest. He experiences a sensation like hunger. But he knows he is not hungry. On a dark path, the prince encounters a wolf.]

10.

I have seen wolves in reality. Perhaps at a zoo. I don't remember. Regardless, the figure the prince encounters in the forest isn't meant to represent an actual wolf. The figure is, instead, meant to represent what is known in a nearby village as the Loup-Garou. The Loup-Garou is a creature from folklore.

11.

Folklore is a closed system that bears no relationship to reality.

12.

I will record two facts about this creature. The first fact is that the Loup-Garou is a man who has the ability to change himself into a wolf at will. The second fact is that, if someone encounters a Loup-Garou, he must not say anything about the encounter to anyone, or he *himself* will be transformed into a wolf for the rest of his days.

13.

Furthermore [the prince knows the lore about the Loup-Garou. One of the knights in the castle told the prince the story. The knight heard the story in the village.]

14.

I imagine this knight to be handsome. He has blond hair on his chest. He is clean-limbed. The knight and the prince have been together in the dark halls of the castle, unbeknownst to the prince's wife. The knight and the prince have made love. They have made love a great many times, in fact. Once, the castle dogs came to lick the semen from the bellies of the knight and prince. The two men laughed. After that, the knight told the prince about the Loup-Garou while they held each other on a secret bed of straw in a long empty chamber of the castle.

15.

Now [in the forest, the prince sees the creature. Only the creature isn't what the prince imagined when the knight told the story. The Loup-Garou looks nothing like a wolf or even a dog. Instead, it looks like a man, a tall and muscular man, with a dark thatch of hair on his chest and another thatch of hair around his cock. The Loup-Garou has a long cock and full-looking testicles. His thighs are flanks of muscle].

16.

A question could be asked: how does the prince recognized the figure in the forest as the Loup-Garou if the Loup-Garou looks nothing like what the prince imagined? How does the prince know this isn't simply a naked man? In order to answer that question, it is important to remember the Loup-Garou is a creature from folklore, a figure rendered. It is also important to remember I am not actually sure I like sex. I enjoy imagining sex, most definitely. I enjoyed imagining the sex between the prince and the knight, for instance. I liked picturing the two of them together in the dark rooms of the castle. I liked picturing the two men kissing and stroking one another and promising never to leave each other's side.

17.

My intention, when I began this story, was for the prince and the Loup-Garou to have sex in the forest. It was going to be rough sex. The kind of sex one might have with a wolf from folklore. But now, instead of imagining sex between the prince and the Loup-Garou, I'm thinking about my actual relationship to sex. I don't think the prince and the Loup-Garou are going to have sex. Perhaps the prince imagines sex in the forest, but he doesn't actually have sex with the Loup-Garou.

18.

I want to say: Sex between two men is a closed system that bears no relationship to reality.

19.

So [the prince and the Loup-Garou stare at one another on a dim-lit path in the woods. The Loup-Garou has menacing yellow eyes. The prince realizes he must escape. He longs to see the blond knight again. He longs to see the castle. Simultaneously, however, he realizes that, if he escapes, he can never mention this encounter to the knight or to anyone else because, if he does, he'll be transformed into a wolf for the rest of his days].

20.

Neither the prince nor the Loup-Garou moves from their spots in the forest.

21.

The prince realizes if he does not move, there will be no chance he could accidently mention this encounter to anyone. He will not risk the possibility of being turned into a wolf. He will not risk the possibility his wife will discover his affair with the knight. He will not risk the possibility the knight will discover his imagined affair with the Loup-Garou.

22.

A question could be asked: Why does the Loup-Garou remain frozen on the forest path along with the prince? Why doesn't this creature lunge at the prince and sink his teeth into the man's soft flesh? Why doesn't the Loup-Garou, who is neither a man nor a wolf nor a figure in reality, simply devour the prince? Does he know something about the system that we do not? Does he understand its relationship to reality? Does the Loup-Garou shift his yellow eyes, from time to time, to look at us? Does he see us standing here at the edge of the path? Does he see how we are frozen too?

Gilgamesh and Enkidu

The raft moves slow upon the river, Gilgamesh at its stern, dressed in the robes of his station; he guides the vessel with a wooden oar. Enkidu, the wild man, rests upon the raft, long-haired, broad-shouldered, dressed in the skins of animals. His fingers trail in the water. He observes the flowers on the riverbank. They shine like funeral lamps in the evening light. "This river—" Enkidu says. "It is that," Gilgamesh replies, sounding weary, "a river." "Are you going to tell me where we are now?" Enkidu asks. "I will," Gilgamesh says. "Once we are clear of this place." "Is it a bad place?" Enkidu asks. "Is it like the Forest of Humbaba?" "No," Gilgamesh says. "It's only a river." Enkidu shifts his body. The raft rocks beneath him. He is glad to be, once more, with Gilgamesh. "If you're not going to tell me where we are, let's at least play a game," Enkidu says. "As we used to." "All right. A game," Gilgamesh says. "Do you remember the first dream you had about me?" Enkidu asks. Gilgamesh pauses his oar. "I suppose I remember it well enough." "Recite it for me," Enkidu says. "You already know how it goes," Gilgamesh replies. "Please," Enkidu says. Gilgamesh sighs. "There were stars. And stars belonged to me." "How did you know they belonged to you?" Enkidu asks. "The way one knows such things in a dream," Gilgamesh says. "I never know anything in dreams," Enkidu says. "As I stood looking up at the stars," Gilgamesh says, "a skybolt fell upon me." Enkidu smiles at this. "A skybolt, yes, a word for lightning." "A magnificent bolt, flung down," Gilgamesh says. "The skybolt struck me. It made me feel as if—" Enkidu lifts his large hand from the river. He puts it on Gilgamesh's bare thigh. Gilgamesh cries out. "Your hand is cold," he says. "Your leg is warm," Enkidu replies. Gilgamesh dips his oar in the river once again. "Do you remember the second dream you had about me?" Enkidu asks. "Enkidu—" "Well, do you?" "Yes, I remember all my dreams." "I don't believe that," Enkidu says. The wild man props himself on his elbow and peers at the riverbank. "Those strange flowers—" he says. "How long was I sleeping, Gilgamesh?" "A long time," Gilgamesh replies. "Too long." Enkidu closes his eyes. "I remember—before I fell asleep—you told me you loved me." Gilgamesh nods. "As a man loves his wife," Gilgamesh says. "I don't like it when you use those words," Enkidu says. "I know." "Then why do you say them?" Gilgamesh is silent, but he too is now smiling. Enkidu splashes water at him. "Where are we? Tell me. Is this the plain of Lebabon?" "It is not." "This river—" Enkidu says. He pauses. "Yes," Gilgamesh replies. "This river." "I remember your third dream," Enkidu says. "Heaven cried out," he says. "Day grew silent and darkness emerged." "Darkness, yes," Gilgamesh says. Enkidu grows quiet. "This is not the land of the Scorpion Men, is it, Gilgamesh?" he asks finally. "No, Enkidu, it is not." "I can still hear the words you spoke before I fell off to sleep," Enkidu says. "They echo, as if from deep inside a cave. 'My friend whom I love, whom I love so much, the fate of mortals has conquered you.'" "Don't—" Gilgamesh says, sounding pained. "This is the last country, isn't it?" Enkidu says. "I have died and you have come to rescue me, as if from the monster, Humbaba, or the fierce Bull of Heaven. You have come to rescue me and bring me back." "No, Enkidu." Enkidu raises up on the raft. "No?" "I *did* come," Gilgamesh says. "But I've learned we cannot leave this country, this last country. There is no way to do so. And so—" "And so?" "We go deeper. Rest now my friend. We go deeper." Enkidu lays his head upon the raft. His eyes are open. His body, stiff and gray. As night falls, the river descends and the walls of a gorge rise. Gilgamesh continues to steer. Finally, the raft comes to what appears to be a great door standing in the river. The door shimmers like water. There are carvings. Gilgamesh finds he cannot decipher the meaning of the carvings. He does not speak. There is no one to speak to. He hopes only that the door will open.

Man with Pillow

Max couldn't sleep. It seemed he could never sleep these days. And he often found himself lying awake, wondering why. But, tonight, he didn't have to wonder. Tonight, Max knew exactly why he couldn't fall asleep. He'd heard a sound in the hallway beyond the bedroom. And before he allowed himself to drift off, he wanted to make sure he didn't hear the sound again. Finally, after listening for a long while and hearing nothing, Max whispered: "James, are you awake?" James was Max's boyfriend. He was asleep on the other side of the bed with a pillow over his face. James always slept like that because of something that had happened in his childhood. He wouldn't tell Max exactly what that something was, but he said it was bad. And clearly it still bothered James because, at almost thirty, he continued to sleep with a pillow over his face. "James," Max said again, this time nudging James with his foot.

"What?" James said finally, his voice muffled by the pillow.

"I heard a sound," Max said.

"Okay."

"No, really," Max said. "Out in the hall."

James removed the pillow from his face and turned toward Max. His eyes remained closed. "What kind of sound?"

"A footstep, I think," Max said.

James opened his eyes and peered at Max in the darkness. "You heard one footstep?"

"Yes."

"I don't think that's how footsteps work," James said.

Max had known James was going to make a joke. He always joked when he wasn't interested in talking. And more often than not these days, James made jokes.

"I want to check to make sure it was nothing," Max said.

"It *was* nothing," James replied.

"Don't go back to sleep until I'm done looking though, okay?"

"Okay." James closed his eyes and put the pillow back over his face.

Max slipped out of bed and went to the closed bedroom door. He turned the knob slowly. The hallway beyond the bedroom was dark, but Max saw the man almost immediately. The man was tall, dressed in jeans and a black t-shirt. He stood a little more than halfway down the hall. Max could tell the man was gazing at him, even though he couldn't see the man's face. The reason Max couldn't see the man's face was because the man was holding a white bedroom pillow over it. The man stood very still and stiffly posed. Max wanted to scream, to call for James. But he felt sure a scream would cause the man with the pillow to take some sort of action. The man might drop the pillow and run at Max. He might wrap his fingers around Max's throat. Or he might have knife or something worse than a knife. So, instead of yelling, Max slowly closed the bedroom door. There was no lock on the door. And none of the furniture in the room was heavy enough to block it other than the bed. "James," Max whispered now that the door was closed.

James was asleep, holding the pillow to his face.

Max pressed his back against the door. "James," he whispered again, more desperately this time.

Suddenly, James sat up. He tossed the pillow across the room at Max. It struck the wall and landed near Max's feet.

James looked scared. "I had a dream," he said. "Someone was in the hall."

"There *is* someone in the hall," Max whispered.

James furrowed his brow. He looked as if he wasn't fully awake. "What?"

"I just saw him," Max said. "There's a man in the hall. We have to call the police."

James grabbed his cellphone from the nightstand, but instead of dialing, he merely rested the phone in his lap. The expression on his face changed, becoming more relaxed. "You're trying to mess with me, aren't you?" he said. "You know something about what happened to me when I was a kid."

Max shook his head. "You never told me."

James put the phone back on the nightstand. "I think we should do what we did in my dream."

"What did we do?" Max asked, still picturing the man standing stiffly in the shadows of the hall, pressing the pillow to his face.

"We both went back to sleep," James said. "We're both asleep now."

"No—" Max said. "James."

But James was already resting his head against the mattress. He took the pillow from Max's side of the bed and pressed it to his face. "We're asleep," he said. "Trust me."

Max wasn't sure what to do. He knelt down and picked up the pillow James had thrown at him. Then, with his back still against the door, Max pressed the pillow to his own face.

Max stood there like that for a moment.

Inside the pillow, Max saw a bedroom. It was exactly like Max and James' own bedroom only the door to the hall was open again.

The hallway inside the pillow was empty.

The man with the pillow over his face had gone away.

Max felt relieved at first. But then he realized he would eventually have to remove the pillow from his face. He would have to open the real door to the real hallway.

The man would still be there.

And maybe the man would have removed the pillow from his own face.

Maybe the man beneath the pillow would look like James. Or maybe he'd look like Max. Or just maybe he'd look like both of them. And the man would say: "James was right, you know? You're both dreaming." He'd point to the bed where two men lay asleep, not touching each other. Never touching each other these days. And he'd say, "Do you know what happens when two men have the same dream?"

And Max would search for an answer because he knew he had to provide one for the man in the hall. But he wouldn't find the right words. He wouldn't find *any* words, in fact.

Because how could there be an answer for a question like that?

Mars, 1887

The sky is dark. The sun is dark.

Rusted hills stand in a half-circle like mourners at a funeral.

Captain Phillips orders us to take the airship and explore the dry canal bed near the western perimeter of the encampment. "To its source," the captain says. As if a dry canal might have a source. As if he believes such a thing. The captain comes to us from the Woolrich Academy in London and speaks with the confidence of such a man. Yet his expression betrays another state. He too is beginning to lose faith in the queen's geographers. And like the rest of us, he fears we will not find water here.

Lieutenant Dawes assumes the airship's controls, and I am seated beside him, glad the two of us have been sent on a mission alone. I have not yet had the chance to speak with the lieutenant at length. He was not part of our original battalion. But he is quite handsome. Even in the dust, he is handsome: green eyes, thick blond mustache.

He adjusts the airship's controls.

Together we drift over barren fields, orange and crimson. The dry Martian canal bed curves below.

When I speak, I taste salt on my lips. "Lewis's theory," I say. "What do you think of it, lieutenant? That there might be men or something like men..."

Lieutenant Dawes gazes out the front-facing porthole. At first, I think he might not answer my question. But then, he clears his throat. "I don't think there's anyone, John," he says.

I nod. He knows my name. And he uses it without my rank. I find this curious, but I also find I am glad for such familiarity.

I look out the front-facing porthole.

The red landscape appears folded, crushed.

"You were stationed near Brixton," I say.

Lieutenant Dawes makes a sound that might indicate affirmation.

"Families are often stationed near—" I say.

"I don't have a family," he replies.

"Ah." I feel embarrassed. Lieutenant Dawes is likely a private man. I try to think of something else to say. Something that might cover over my mistake. "Were you an athlete at school?"

"I was," Lieutenant Dawes says.

"And what game did you play?"

He hesitates. Perhaps the lack of water is affecting his thoughts, slowing them, as it is with the other men. "Rugby," he says finally.

"The others were talking about rugby earlier," I say. "They wanted to set up a pitch to distract themselves. The captain forbids it, of course."

"Of course," he says.

"Well," I say, "you do have the look of a rugger."

Lieutenant Dawes nods.

"I was never any good at sports," I say. "I tried my hand at painting. My subject was Mars, actually. I started painting when they were testing the first ships. We could see them in the sky above Bexley—that's where I lived when I was a boy. I dreamed of Mars, the landscapes. And I hoped I would come one day here. I thought I could live differently in this place. Do you know what I mean?"

"Amongst men," Lieutenant Dawes says.

"That's right. Amongst men."

Silence falls between us. The airships engines drone.

"What did it look like?" Lieutenant Dawes asks after a time. "The Mars in your dreams."

I feel embarrassed. Still, I tell him the truth. The men in our encampment are all beginning to look so hollow and weak; it makes me want to tell the truth at every turn. "Mars was covered in flowers," I say. "White flowers. And there were green hills too. Like the hills in Saint James Park near Piccadilly."

Lieutenant Dawes nods slowly again.

"I was foolish to believe it would be like that," I say, pausing to think of the white flowers in my paintings. I wonder if, as a boy, I'd been painting funeral flowers. "So were you at Harrow then? Is that where you played rugby?"

"I don't want to talk about rugby," he says.

"I'm sorry," I say. "Is there something else you'd like to talk about?"

"Not yet," he says.

"Yet?"

"That's right."

Before I can think of another question, I realize we are no longer travelling along the dry canal bed as Captain Phillips ordered. Instead, we are moving over a series of rolling pink hills. The shadows here grow lean.

"Did we lose sight of the canal?" I ask.

Lieutenant Dawes clears this throat. It must be dry indeed.

"Should I consult the map?" I say, reaching for the compartment where such things are stowed.

"I have something to show you," Lieutenant Dawes replies.

"How's that?"

"I went exploring yesterday."

"Alone?"

"That's right," Lieutenant Dawes says. "I went out in the evening, as the sun was setting."

This makes little sense to me. No one is to go exploring alone. And no one is to go out in the cold of the evening.

"How did you acquire a ship?" I ask.

"I took it," he says.

"But didn't anyone notice?"

"They didn't."

"Well, what did you find?"

"I'm going to show you now," he says. "We're almost there."

I look through the front-facing porthole.

We are drifting toward one of the low Martian hills. It's red and weatherworn. As we draw closer, I realize it isn't a hill at all. Impossibly, it appears to be a kind of pyramid, a stepped ziggurat. The surface of the ziggurat is carved with a complicated pattern that appears to represent human figures, bodies intertwined. I see legs and arms, heads. The sculptures give the impression that a hundred men have climbed the pyramid, covered it, forming a kind of lacework.

"My God," I say.

Dawes says nothing in return.

"But, didn't you tell the captain?"

"I didn't," Dawes replies.

"This is, Lieutenant, this is a discovery of great . . . it proves Lewis's theory, doesn't it? That there are men or something like men . . ."

"I wanted to show you," Lieutenant Dawes says.

"But why would you want to show me?"

He's settling the airship gently on the soil near the structure. Fine dust rises.

"I've watched you," he says.

The ship's doors open. The air outside smells burnt.

The idea that Dawes has been watching me just as I have been watching him is almost too much to bear, especially in this moment. "But—" I say, gazing up at the stone bodies on the ziggurat.

Lieutenant Dawes climbs out of the ship and walks toward the structure. There is an aperture at its base, an open door.

I hurry after him.

We pass through the low door and find ourselves in a dark hall. I have little time to study the carvings here. But there *are* carvings, I can see that. More stone bodies. They appear to embrace, limbs linked, torsos pressed. At times, they even dissolve into one another.

I follow Dawes.

The tunnel cants downward. The space inside the ziggurat grows darker still.

"Lieutenant?" I say.

"Let me light a lamp," he says.

There is movement in the darkness to my left. Then the space brightens.

Dawes holds one of the brass-handled box lamps from our encampment.

"Where did you get that?" I say.

"I brought it with me when I went exploring yesterday. I left it here."

The space around us, a large stone room, is empty. Walls tilt toward the apex of the ziggurat. For a moment, I feel dizzy.

Lieutenant Dawes unbuttons his red military jacket. He removes it and places it on the floor.

I think, at first, that he must be overheated, though the chamber itself is quite cool.

Then he is unbuttoning his shirt as well.

He removes the shirt.

I see a tuft of blond hair on his narrow chest.

My heart stutters.

Lieutenant Dawes folds his shirt and places it on top of his uniform jacket.

He begins to unfasten the clasps of his woolen trousers.

"Lieutenant?" I say.

He looks at me, eyes red rimmed, cheeks pallid. I wonder if he's been drinking his water rations. It's my understanding some of the men have been saving theirs, even the men who are white-lipped and weak. They want the reassurance there is still water to be had. I wonder if lack of water could have caused a kind of mania in Lieutenant Dawes.

"What's the matter?" he says.

"I—"

Dawes is in his undergarments now. He's thinner than I imagined. I see the outline of his stiffened member through his long johns.

"We should return to the camp," I say, though I'm not sure if I mean this.

"We'll go back soon enough," Dawes replies.

He is naked then. His member, swollen, reddish. Nearly the color of Mars itself.

Dawes lies down on his back on the stone floor of the angular room and gazes at me.

I do not speak. I am afraid that if I do it will break whatever spell or madness has overtaken the lieutenant.

I begin taking off my boots, my trousers, my jacket.

Unclothed, I go to Dawes.

I stand over him.

"I have—I've never done any of this," I say.

Dawes takes my hand. He pulls me gently, touching my leg and then my hip.

I straddle the lieutenant. He rubs the tip of his member against me until we are both wet. Then he is inside me.

There is pain at first.

I look down into his green eyes.

Lieutenant Dawes stares, not at me, but at some point on the high ceiling.

I wish he would look at me.

I want to ask him to do so.

Dawes' hips move under me. As he thrusts, the walls of the ziggurat seem to lengthen. The ceiling is now impossibly high.

Lieutenant Dawes is deep inside me.

The pain changes, becoming something better.

"Dawes," I whisper.

He does not reply but continues to move his hips.

"Dawes," I say again.

This is what it feels like, I think. *This is what it feels like to—*

Then, in that moment, I cannot hold my essence inside the frame of my body. My bones will no longer keep me in their cage. I feel as though my spirit is falling upward, pouring out of the top of my skull.

My vantage changes.

I drift somewhere above.

In the yellow light of the lantern, I see Lieutenant Dawes' white naked form. I see my own smaller frame as well, straddling him still.

Lieutenant Dawes' hands clutch my hips.

His rhythmic movements grow more vigorous. I see my own head tilt back.

Then Lieutenant Dawes slows, ceasing his thrusts.

His member slips out of me. I know I am wet with him, his milk.

This is what it feels like, I think, as I look down at myself and Lieutenant Dawes. We both lie on the stone floor.

I find I am not frightened.

Lieutenant Dawes stares up at the apex of the ziggurat. I realize he is staring up at me. He has been staring at me the entire time. He knows I am floating here near the ceiling of the pyramid. Somehow, he knows.

"All of the other men . . ." Lieutenant Dawes says, swallowing dryly. My body lies limp beside him. "There is no water for them," he says. "There will be no water. There's only this. It's all we have to offer."

I find I cannot reply. I continue to float there above us both. There are more figures carved into the stone at the apex of the ziggurat. The figures do not move. They do not turn their heads. But I understand they are watching me.

I try to remember when Lieutenant Dawes came to our battalion from Brixton. I try to remember the first time I saw him.

That there are men, I think, *or something like men*.

I shift in the darkness at the apex, drifting toward the stone figures. They have not moved. And yet they seem to reach their hands toward me.

Lieutenant Dawes strokes my cheek on the floor below. "You were right about one thing, John," he says. "There were flowers here once. Whole fields of them."

Genesis

The Paradise is small and spherical in shape. There are plants with large flowers. The petals of the flowers are suggestive of flesh. There is a narrow river with clear water. Two men live inside the Paradise. They live alone. They eat the flowers that look like flesh. They drink water from the clear river. Both men are naked. They have sex often and in different ways. Sometimes, the men rub their cocks together until they ejaculate. At other times, one man will put his cock inside the other and rub until both men ejaculate. After sex, the two men walk the Paradise. They talk about what they see: the flowers, the clear river, the smallness of the world. One day a god comes to the Paradise. The god looks something like a tree, but not exactly. There are branches, yes. And there is a trunk with bark. But there are no leaves or fruits of any kind. The two men look at the god. The god looks back at the two men. Then the god departs. The two men have sex again. This time, it's different. Not worse. Just different. After sex, they walk around the Paradise. They walk for a long time before either of them speaks. One of the men finally pauses near the narrow river and says, "What if I make up a story for you?" The other man doesn't answer at first. He wonders what kind of story it might be. He wonders if he's ever heard a story before. He gazes at the clear river and the flowers. Then he looks at the other man and notices, for the first time, that the man has brown hair and dark eyes. He thinks about the smallness of their world. Then he feels an emotion he can't quite name.

It's something like confusion, but not exactly that. Finally, he says, "All right. Go ahead. Tell your story." He can't help himself.

The Pleasure Garden

London, 1732

1.

George tells ghost stories as we cross the black river.

2.

The ferry is lamplit. Nearly empty at this late hour.

3.

George is my classmate at Marlwood. And though he never paid me much of any mind, he's invited me to go with him to the gardens at Vauxhall.

4.

My sister has been to Vauxhall. She's been everywhere in London. When she was drunk one night, she told me what men do together on the dark and winding paths of the pleasure garden. "They go there to be wanton, Jack," she said. "They wrestle each other to the ground. One might press his lips to another's mouth. Stick his tongue inside. There's more than that too. I've seen it."

5.

George himself is handsome. He plays cricket and boxes in the bareknuckle fights. I've watched him often from afar. His body is long and hard. But his mouth looks soft. And though he smells of bitter smoke, there's something sweet about him too.

6.

I hope George might mean to wrestle me to the ground on one of old quiet paths at the garden. Maybe he'll press his mouth to mine in the shadows of the mirror house. Or we'll lie together on the banks of the floating island and listen to the distant violin drifting down from the great hall.

7.

Vauxhall is made for all sorts of pleasures.

8.

Yet, as we cross the river, George gives no sign of any such intention. Instead he continues to talk of ghosts: "There's one that creeps about the supper boxes near the Turkish tent," George says. "He bothers the diners there."

I lean toward George, hoping a strong wave might knock me into his lap.

"He's what's called the Brown-Paper Man," George continues. "Old fellow. Dressed in a suit of burned newsprint. He approaches men and women and begs for coins. But coins aren't what really he wants."

"What does he want?" I ask softly.

George takes a wooden pipe from the pocket of his coat. "I couldn't say exactly, Jack. But those who've seen his face say, well, they say it's odd. For he looks as if he's made of brown paper too."

9.

I move one knee carefully toward George.

10.

"Then there's him who's called the Headless Bear," George says.

"A bear?" I say, glancing toward the far river bank where torches glow dimly about the black gates of the pleasure garden. There is no moon. Faint music, likely from a band of roaming minstrels, drifts toward us across the water.

"It's some poor creature left over from the king's hunt," George says. "Poachers took the bear's head. Now the body wanders all about, walking on its two hind feet through the woods."

11.

Fire brightens George's eyes as he lights his pipe.

12.

"There's one more too," George says.

"What's this one called?" I ask.

"Well, he doesn't have a proper name. And he's not really a ghost at all, I suppose."

"What then?"

George leans close, but not close enough to touch me. "It's one of the fair boys, I've heard," he says. "Come down from the Summer Court."

"What's the Summer Court?" I say.

George blows a ring of smoke. "You know the answer well enough, don't you, Jack?"

I consider this, then shake my head.

"What season is it now, Jack?" George asks.

"The season when the leaves fall," I say.

George nods. "That's right. And the fair boys of the Summer Court have to find somewhere to go, don't they? There's no more dew to drink or soft flowers to rest their heads upon."

13.

I look toward the far bank again. The black gates of Vauxhall loom closer still. Dark and glittering in the torchlight.

14.

"We should have come to the gardens in the summer, you know?" George says. "We could have had a time together then. But traipsing around in the cold and the fallen leaves, that's no such thing for you, Jack."

"I don't mind," I say. "I'm hearty enough."

"No," George says, resting the stem of his pipe on his lower lip. "You're not. I've watched you at school."

"You have?" I say.

George nods. "You never play sports."

"No," I say.

"And I've seen you watching me," George says.

"Have you?"

15.

I think of my sister then. She said her own young suitor, Mr. Brenner, was so sweet to her at the pleasure gardens. She said he took her hand and kissed it lightly. He picked daisies for her from a spot near the bathing pond.

16.

I study George as he smokes, the sinewy strength of him.

17.

"My sister tells me men wrestle each other on the paths at Vauxhall," I say.

"Wrestle?" George says, raising his brow.

I nod. "And they do other things too."

"Is that so?" George says, blowing smoke. Then, he sits silent for a time. Finally, he says, "We're not going to wrestle, Tom."

"No," I say. "I didn't think so."

18.

"So many ghosts at Vauxhall," George says.

It sounds like it, I want to reply. But instead I say nothing.

19.

Soon, our ferry knocks against the wooden dock on the far side of the river.

20.

George's hand is on my shoulder then.

21.

His fingers are far colder than I imagined them to be.

It's Later Than You Think

When I was dead, I returned to my father's house, an old farmstead in Northwestern Ohio, and I stood alone in the gravel drive, satisfied to see that the house was just as I remembered it—small and gray, rising on a plot of land west of a moonlit apple orchard. I had not been to my father's house for some ten years because Los Angeles, where I lived, was so far from Ohio. But I'd never doubted that I would return to the place where I'd once played with the old farm dog and climbed the big tree to sit on a branch and call down to my father from the leaves as if I'd become invisible. I did not knock on the door of the house because only a stranger would knock, and I was no stranger, no matter how long I stayed away. Instead, I walked inside and stood in the dark of the kitchen, listening to the sound of the television and smelling the lingering scent of whatever lonely dish my father had eaten that evening. Then, I went then to the living room and stood in the doorway until my father, who sat watching television, glanced up. His smile was almost the same as it had been ten years ago, though perhaps slightly altered by the passage of time. I wondered if I looked older too. More than that, I wondered if I looked as though I had died. Was I pale? Disheveled? My father stood from his chair and walked toward me, moving slower than he once had, and he put his arms around me and said my name. I hugged him. My father didn't ask why I carried no luggage; instead, he said, I didn't know you were coming. I would have picked you up at the airport. I would have driven you. And I said I wanted to surprise him, and he asked me if I was hungry. I said I was not, remembering the last thing I'd eaten, a turkey sandwich with no mustard and no mayonnaise. The bread had been dry. The sandwich remained in my stomach and would probably always remain there. And my father asked me to come and sit with him. Unless you're tired, he said. If you're tired, I'll go upstairs and make your bed. I just washed some sheets. But I was not tired, and I did not want to go bed, so, instead, I sat with my father and we talked for a time about Los Angeles and what was happening there, and then we watched what was on the television, and my father fell asleep in his chair; he snored as he slept, and I smiled at this because I remembered how he used to snore when I was very young. And I looked around the room, shining the lights of my eyes over everything, soft yellow lights, casting shadows, black shadows.

An Orgy

Rome, 38 CE

The colors of marble: blonde, lilac, green, rosy yellow and white. It happens in the forest. Late evening. The ilex are dark here, like tarnished mirrors. There is a ruin. A place of sacrifice. Asphodels grow, glowing, holy. The men, for they are all men, come silently in soft raiment. There is wine, a great deal it, from the cellars of the one who calls himself *Il Sodoma*, the Sodomite. Someone whispers he knows what dying would feel like: *a return to a place where one is wanted.* The men are red lipped by the time it begins. Bodies pale in the antique light. Pieces of a moving statuary. Their roles are not announced. But such things are understood. Some men are penetrated. Others are not. All of them kneel in soft blankets of pine needles. There is a sound in the forest, a crying. In their collective thoughts: flights of black stairs, blue wind flowers, a song, complex yet primitive. Semen is spilled. Afterwards, the men lay together. The gods go walking.

The Coil

Arthur awakes in the golden wood. He dreamed of a silver cup or a stone that fell from the sky. He cannot remember which, and he wonders if such things can be said to matter any longer. The campfire has gone out. His bedroll is covered in morning dew. He watches mistletoe flutter on the branch of a tall birch and listens to the bright song of a jay. The journey, he realizes, is ending. Two weeks out, and nearly done. The forest seems as if it might close around him like a giant eye. Soon there will only be the memory of these travels. Half-invented tales told to other men in a shadowed hall. Arthur stands and makes his way toward the stream near the encampment, careful not to wake Sir Guyon. The knight looks handsome there in his own bedroll—tangle of yellow hair, bristle of a young man's beard. Arthur remembers how the two of them used to play together in the barley fields west of the castle, Fox and Goose and Hoodman's Blind.

Arthur kneels before the stream. Shadows glide across the surface of the water. He knows what must happen next if the quest is to continue (and it *must* continue. He won't go back... not yet). He's learned his occult imagination from the most convincing of prophets. Arthur relaxes his gaze. Blurs his vision. And there, twisting in the ripples of the water, he sees it: a kind of answer. "What have you found, my lord?" Sir Guyon asks, approaching from behind, eyes still bleary from sleep. He wears only breeches and a coarse linen shirt. Arthur pauses and then holds his hand out over the water. Guyon looks down and sees nothing. Of course he doesn't. There's nothing to see. "Darkness," Arthur says, gravely. "A presage."

"Of what?" Guyon asks.

Arthur peers at the water, as if it's become some scryer's stone. "A creature, cruelly scaled and long-bodied," he says. "A devil, of sorts."

Sir Guyon takes a step back, and Arthur is pleased. It's always fear first with the knights, then bravery. He wonders if Guyon has ever been in love. The knight has pretended at such emotion, of course. All of them do. They write letters to maidens in their thick unschooled hand. But has he ever felt what Arthur feels now—the true sting of it?

The serpent, Arthur says, is hidden in a cave on the mountain pass above. Guyon bows his head, lips moving. He speaks to God as only a young man can. Arthur prays too, but not about a dragon. They gather their bedrolls and begin their travels, Guyon always in the lead. Arthur carefully observes the knight's strong neck, the movement of his lean shoulders. He wonders if a quest like this could be made to last forever. Time might swallow them. Their names would appear side by side in ages of poetry. Their souls could mix forever in the higher air.

When they finally reach the cave—for there actually is a cave on the mountain pass, to Arthur's surprise—Guyon draws his broadsword. "Does it sleep, my lord?" Guyon asks.

Dragons are made of sleep, Arthur thinks. For they themselves are dreams. "Sir Guyon," he says, and the knight turns to look at him, clear-eyed and fine. There are too many words behind Arthur's teeth. None of them will come out.

Guyon raises his brow. "What is it, my lord?" he asks.

Arthur shakes his head. "Tread carefully, my friend."

And together they move into the darkness of the cave. Guyon lights a torch, but the flame is dim and only serves to make more shadows. They progress down a narrow passage, and Arthur is reminded of the tombs beneath the castle. This cave smells of death.

"I can hear the monster breathing," Guyon whispers.

Arthur does not want to believe this. He invented the creature after all. He's invented all the fabulous things that populate the quests. None of them are real. There is no vast Green Knight. No ghost-white stag. Such things are extensions of his own passion. Emotion manifest. Another reason to drag Sir Guyon and others like him into the woods.

And yet Arthur too can hear something now, a ragged sound that echoes against the cave walls. The smell of decay mixes with the scent of smoke. Guyon slips on loose stone, and Arthur watches his friend tumble down into a large shallow chamber.

"Here," Guyon hisses, righting himself. "Look, my lord."

But Arthur doesn't need to look. He can feel it. Something has gone wrong. Sir Guyon is advancing on a scaled coil at the center of the stone chamber, excited because, after all this time, he has finally found something to slay. "Wait," Arthur says, but the coil is already unknotting itself there in the dark. Arthur sees a serpent's head. The creature's eyes are nothing like love. They are white. They are blank stones. Like years of waiting. And he wonders what he might do to make this right. Is there a way to kill the thing in his heart before it does what it intends to do?

On Decadence

London, 1893

We eat the tongues of songbirds.

A return to the Hellenic ideal.

Our motto: Lend yourself to your desires.

We are informed by the new sciences: mesmerism, telepathy.

We know the minds of others.

We revel in the ambiguous, the sinister.

Just yesterday, we encountered a bourgeois with a potbelly and thick sideburns. He walked with a cane and a satisfied swagger. We trailed him through the streets of Mayfair, our faces white as plaster. We smiled. Not because we were pleased. But in order to show our distaste.

Imagine the glacial stare of a Dandy. He is always turned out. Never emotionally spontaneous.

We are the sickness of the century.

We are exhausted.

There are many disappointments here.

Many minor degradations.

We smoke a cigarette. And then another.

Our fingertips are yellowed.

We recline on pillows the color of pomegranates.

We seek illusion.

We seek the invention of a Paradise.

At times, we dream of living in an ancient hospital. We want to ramble its empty gray wards. We want the lingering scent of a long-ago death. The filter of cold light from a high window.

We think of King Ludwig of Bavaria. He is said to have built for himself an artificial garden, mechanical animals with amber-glass eyes, a man-made cave encrusted with shining jewels. There was music in his trees. Handsome soldiers dressed as nymphs and satyrs. They cavorted. The king would catch them in the darkness. He kissed them and stroked their well-made bodies.

We find we have come to despise families, mothers and fathers. We despise little children.

We are left limp, used up by life.

We avoid thoughts of the hateful period in which we live. We delve, instead, into the past.

The possibility of marriage is abhorrent to us.

We have lost touch with our school friends. We live in rented rooms above a tavern.

Our family has some wealth. We have no need to find employment.

We hate churches. We hate ministers. We hate candlelight and the middle class.

In coffee houses, we spend our time speaking with darkly attractive young men. We never form relationships, of course. But we like to look into their black eyes. We like to imagine touching their full-lipped mouths.

In those same establishments, we have encountered certain pieces of literature. The dark young men carry pamphlets, the authors of which are unknown to us. The pages contain intricate descriptions of aesthetic pleasures—the distillations of black magicians, the varied scents of burning resins. We find obscure investigations into quintessence. There are interviews with men who claim to have sailed the *mare tenebrarum* and found the "pale continent."

We read too in these pamphlets of the Roman Empire, of Emperor Hadrian. He took a young lover called Antinous, beautiful and firm. The youth drowned one bright afternoon in the Nile. He was found floating, facedown in the rushes. Some days later, Antinous's spirit appeared to Hadrian, a shining vessel, suspended in the air above the river. He was marble-eyed, golden-lipped. The emperor saw this and fell to his knees. He made worship. The men and women of Khartoum fell to their knees and made worship too.

In the margins of these passages, someone has scrawled notes in an unsteady hand:

> *There are gods*, one of the notes says, *but oh, they are not the gods anyone has thought to name.*

We smoke a cigarette.

We consider the meaning of such notes in the pamphlets.

Normally, the notes accompany descriptions of a certain hidden place in London. The place is never named. Yet we have come to recognize its details: a maze of broken columns, subterranean chambers, the smell of myrrh. There is a sound of moving water. This place is haunted by the ancient world and said to be located near the remnants of the old Roman Wall. Several of the hand-written notes repeat two words:

> *Hadrian's Palace.*

We have read descriptions of the palace's great subterranean fountains, the waters of which are dyed black. There are said to be cavernous theaters and rooms where once fine banquets have turned to dust. Men gather in this sunken realm. They speak softly to one another and know each other well.

We think of beautiful Antinous, young lover of the emperor. We picture him floating in the air above the Nile. Holy body. Erotic and divine.

We think of Hadrian and his worship.

We wonder if the emperor might have brought his worship here to London ages ago.

We wonder if the ancient world may still exist somewhere beneath our city's paving stones.

If so, might such a place finally provide the sort of escape we've been searching for?

"Who made the notes in these pamphlets?" we ask one of the dark young men at the coffee house.

"Notes?" he says. He sips his black coffee and looks at us with black eyes.

We nod. "The hurried ones," we say. "Here." We point to the cramped handwriting in the pamphlet's margin.

The dark young man gazes at the writing and then the answer comes: "Ephraim," he says. "Ephraim made the notes."

"And where is Ephraim now?" we ask.

"He's dead," the dark young man says.

"Dead? How did he die?"

The dark young man shrugs. "How does anyone die?"

We steal one of the pamphlets and read the scribbled notes carefully. We walk the streets near the Roman Wall, searching for some entrance to the sunken realm. We listen for the sounds of moving water and try to catch the scent of Myrrh. And yet, nothing is revealed to us but the monotony of the present moment, the endless thrum of the dull city.

We find ourselves hungering for Hadrian's Palace more and more. For secrecy and worship. For camaraderie in the dust.

We do not return to the coffee house for several weeks.

Our father visits our rented room.

He angers us with dinners and common talk of sales and finance. He tells us how our brothers and sisters are faring (they are, of course, faring well).

We eat the tongues of song birds, we remind ourselves. *A return to the Hellenic ideal.*

When, finally, we visit the coffee house once more, there is something different in the air. The dark young men who gather there do not speak to one another. They do not read their pamphlets where the descriptions of Hadrian's Palace are written. We ask one of them what has happened. (Is this perhaps the same young man we spoke to weeks before?) He points to a dim table in one corner of the room. At the table sits another young man, all alone. His head is lowered. His clothes are ragged. And his big hands, the color of ivory, are folded on the tabletop. "He has returned," the young man says to us.

"Who has returned?" we ask.

"Ephraim," he says.

"But I was told Ephraim was dead."

The young man nods. "We believed he was."

We go to the table of the young man in ragged clothes. We sit in the seat opposite him. "Are you Ephraim?" we say.

His raises his head slowly to gaze at us.

We are afraid when we see his eyes, his lips.

Ephraim is dead, we think. And then: *How does anyone die?*

We know we must be bold. We must remember our purpose. Ephraim made the notes in the pamphlets.

And even though we are afraid, we ask him: "Where is it? Where is Hadrian's Palace?"

The young man shows yellow teeth. A secret smile. An awful thing.

"You know my name..." he says haltingly. His voice is deep. Like something buried in the earth.

"Ephraim," we say. "Your name is Ephraim. Please, we are tired."

"*I* was tired," Ephraim says.

"We are tired of London," we say. "Sick of the age. We want an escape. A return to—"

"*I* wanted escape," Ephraim says.

We wonder if he is mocking us. "And you found it, didn't you?" we say.

"I found it," Ephraim says.

"Yes," we say. "But where?"

He lowers his head to stare at the tabletop once more.

We want to reach out, to touch his ivory-colored hand and rouse him, but we fear the hand would be cold.

"Tell us please," we say. "Tell us where to find Hadrian's Palace."

Ephraim makes a strange clicking sound with his teeth.

His tongue lolls from his mouth. It is the color of blood.

"I was tired," he says again. "I was tired."

We think, for a moment, we hear the sound of a distant river, the movement of its waters. We imagine the dead youth, Antinous, his spirit hovering in the air, marble-eyed and golden-lipped.

An odd noise issues from Ephraim's throat, a kind of rattle.

Frightened, we stand and walk toward the door of the coffee house. We tell ourselves the dark young men have nothing more to offer us. We do not need their pamphlets. We do not need instructions. We will find Hadrian's Palace on our own. We will find it this very night, in fact.

We eat the tongues of songbirds, we think. *A return to the Hellenic ideal.*

Fog has shrouded London's streets. We can barely see the lampposts.

We turn to look behind us.

We turn because we are still frightened.

Is there someone following in the distance, shuffling quickly toward us now?

There are gods, we think. *But oh, they are not the gods anyone has thought to name.*

Wolves Can Be Mistaken

From the Diary of King James VI
13 January 1581

A young man scales the tower now nearly every night, entering my sleeping chamber through the high window there. I recognize him as a witch, for he has no weight and floats, as if through strange ether, over the heavy oaken chair and the trunk from days at Agincourt. His handsomeness is such that I cannot fathom it written upon a man. The boy's hair is white, and his eyes, a dark yellow. He crawls into my bed, smelling of smoke and cedar, and he talks to me in a low voice as the tallow candle gutters on the stand. He tells me there are wolves in the forest near the castle and they have learned to speak. I ask him what the wolves say, and he tells me they talk of Christ. "But what could wolves know of our Lord?" I say, half-afraid. The young man licks his teeth. He says the wolves know Christ was not a man. He was, instead, the limb of a much larger form. The wolves have travelled back along the limb and seen the great body for themselves. They have crawled upon its broad chest. And they have seen its grinning face. "The face of God?" I ask. The witch boy kisses me then gently on the mouth. "Not God," he says. His lips taste of acorns. He runs his dark tongue along my neck and reaches beneath the blanket to hold my swollen cock. The wolves live in a cave full of rubies, he says. They sleep there amongst the stones and dream of the great body. They call it Time, but it is not exactly Time. He strokes my cock, slowly at first and then faster, and soon I am with him in the forest, gliding amongst the shadows of the black trees. Together, we make the pattern of a serpent. He calls me his innocence. And he laughs as we fly.

Notes on the Heavens

Hollywood, 1907

1.

Field of grape vines. Crooked lime trees. A grove of painted oranges.

2.

Hollywoodland, as it is sometimes called, lies west of the river, silent and sun-bleached. A post office. A small hotel (like a mission church). Two markets and a single streetcar. The streetcar rattles dust along the boulevard.

3.

Motion picture men come here from the East. It's said they want to escape the tyranny of Thomas Edison and his "rules of production."

4.

Mr. Harvey Wilcox, town founder, is a thin man who lost the use of legs some years ago to typhoid. Now, instead of rolling about in a chair, he can be seen strapped and standing in a pair of tin legs, pushed along by an Ecuadorian dressed in white linen. Mr. Wilcox shouts orders to the men breaking ground for his new hotel, The Cecil.

5.

I have been hired, in my capacity, to investigate an odd acre that stands some miles south of Hollywood. It is the supposed location of a commune known as Der Himmel (from the German, "The Heavens").

6.

The man who hired me is in search of his son, Thomas Whitmore. The boy was a hopeful and handsome youth who came to Hollywood to see about working in the new pictures. Having no luck with that, he went off to Der Himmel to do whatever a man might do down there. His father has not heard from him since.

7.

Noon. The day of my arrival. I interview the wife of Mr. Harvey Wilcox in the tea garden of the old hotel. She wears a yellow dress with a high stiff collar. A shade tree looms over her. The tree is covered in pink blossoms that look like human faces. "A German," Mrs. Wilcox says, moving the warm air with a Japanese fan. "That's who it was that bought up all the land to the south. My husband was not pleased, Mr. Samuels. Not one bit. People said the German built a little town down there. He had an old stone village and a snowcapped mountain and a miniature castle too. All fitted out to look just like it was in Germany. But, soon enough, others started saying that wasn't true at all. There was nothing down there to the south but fig trees. Rows and rows of fig trees. And those who had seen the little castle and the village and the mountain said they couldn't imagine where all of it had gone. Had the old German torn it down during the night? People are so strange here in California, Mr. Samuels. They come for the oddest of reasons. Health cures and love cults. There are even those who believe they might have a chance of meeting men from another planet. Venus is what they say. *Venus!* Isn't that a curious way of thinking?"

8.

After tea, a horse-drawn train takes me south to Der Himmel. I am the only man aboard. The driver wears a burlap sack over his head so as not to breathe the foul dust of the air. We arrive at an iron gate in an open field. Beyond the gate are the fig trees mentioned by Mrs. Harvey Wilcox.

9.

A small red-framed building the size of an outhouse stands near the gate. A very old man with a white beard is asleep inside. I tap on the window of the little house, and the old man awakens in stages. By the time he finally looks at me with odd rheumy eyes, I am not sure if he is actually awake or if I am now located inside one of his crusted dreams.

10.

After some conversation, I am granted permission to enter the grove. I pass through the iron gate. There is no path of any kind. California sun filters down through the fig leaves. A lake glitters in the bright distance.

11.

Halfway to the lake, I hear someone whistling. The tune is one I almost remember.

A tall young man—maybe eighteen or nineteen years of age—appears, pushing a wheelbarrow full of dead tree branches. The branches look like human arms. He's dark-haired and strapping, and he reminds me of someone I once knew. Maybe he looks like one of the young men I befriended during my first years in Chicago. There were so many handsome boys back then. We used to venture out at night to the dance halls on Broadway Street.

I call to the young man through the fig trees.

He lowers his wheelbarrow and turns in a slow circle as if he has no idea where the sound of my voice came from.

"Over here, son," I say.

Finally, the young man sees me.

"I'm wondering if we might talk," I say, walking toward him.

The young man silently raises his work-stained hand, gesturing toward the lake.

We walk together. I glance between the fig trees, trying to see if there's anyone else working in the grove. But we appear to be alone.

The lake is large and calm. We sit on a flat rock beneath a tree. "I'm searching for someone," I say. "A certain Thomas Whitmore. Likely your age. From Chicago. Have you heard of him?"

The young man stares at me. There is something in his eyes not exactly like dread. I realize he does, in fact, look nearly identical to one of the young men I knew in my early days. The boy's name was Samuel. He was the son of a farmer from southern Illinois. He had big shoulders and a gentle smile. We used to joke that, if he married me one day, his name would be Samuel Samuels.

Gazing at the young man in the fig grove, I feel suddenly heavy. And I wonder how many years it's been since I danced with any of those boys in Chicago.

12.

Birds sing in the fig trees. A breeze moves the water of the lake.

13.

"Is this a manmade pond?" I ask the young man after a time.

"What pond?" he says. His voice has a fine timbre.

"Well, right there in front of us," I say, pointing at the lake.

The young man looks at the lake but says nothing.

"Have you ever been to Chicago?" I ask.

"You should probably talk to my boss."

"The old German?"

"He isn't really a German," the young man replies.

"Just point me in the right direction then."

The young man points toward the lake.

14.

I walk to the water's edge. The lake looks as though it's made of quartz. The longer I stare down into the water, the more I begin to realize there might be objects beneath the surface. They're difficult to comprehend at first because of the way the sun plays on the ripples. But, soon, I think I can see a little village sunk beneath the water. And there, in the distance, is a German castle. And beyond the castle is a snow-capped mountain. All of it looks like the memory of a memory. Gray and black, then passing softly into yellow.

15.

I turn to face the young man once more. He raises a big hand to wave at me.

"Are you telling me this doesn't look like a lake to you?" I ask.

The young man says nothing in response.

"Are you Samuel Samuels?" I cannot stop myself from asking this. He looks so much like my old friend I used to dance with. "Or maybe you're the boy called Thomas Whitmore."

"My boss is just up ahead," the young man says. "He'll talk to you."

"I can't go down there," I say. "This is a lake."

"It isn't," the young man replies. "There is no lake here, sir."

16.

I take a step into the water. It's very cold. And I remember those old dance halls on Broadway Street. The way Samuel Samuels and I once moved together. Body against body in the sweating dark. The smell of wheat on his skin. The taste of his neck.

17.

The images beneath the lake begin to flicker as if they are made of light and projected on a screen.

18.

There are people in the little village beneath the lake. I see them now.

Young men and old, all talking together.

I take another step into the cold water in the bright summer sun. And, soon enough, I see Samuel Samuels, my young farm boy, down beneath the water. He's gazing up at me through the ripples. And he looks happy. Thank God. And there is the young Thomas Whitmore too, the boy who disappeared from Hollywood. I recognize him right away. He isn't missing after all.

I take two more steps into the lake.

I see another man, an older fellow, there on the cobbled street of the little village. He's beckoning to me with a gray hand, asking me to come down and talk with him. To walk the streets of the little village at his side.

I turn and look back at the young man on the shore of the lake.

Only it isn't a young man after all, I realize.

It's a fig tree, growing there amongst the rocks.

I take another step into the water.

Marlowe in Love

Deptford, 1593

It was not Christopher Beaston, most famous of the boy actors, with pert lips and amber-colored eyes, who drew our Marlowe's attention. Nor was it Master Cook, nor Master Clarke, nor young Theophilus Bird, all of whom were known to "play the illusion" so expertly when they donned the skirts and coiffed the hair. "These lads appear to lose their cods entirely," wrote George Weston in a private letter to the critic Roger Ascham. And it was true that Beaston and Cook and Clarke could, for a night, transform themselves, becoming Venus and Dido and even Kate the Shrew. John Rainolds, Puritan Father at Hampton Court, would warn of the "filthy sparkles of lust" such boys could engender with their "wanton gestures and bawdy speeches... kissing and bussing their way across the stage." But Marlowe himself paid little mind to either the boy actors or the Puritans. Nor was it the men who worked the brothels of Ram Alley and Little Sodom that drew good Marlowe's passion. The playwright was, of course, known to walk the streets at Whitehall and Seven Dials. He drank in taverns there and kept a certain company with the powdered young men who wore their breeches tight. Marlowe flattered and teased but never touched. Nor did he ask to see any such paramour in private rooms. Marlowe did not love red-haired Thomas Kyd with whom he lived in Shoreditch either. He liked Kyd's writing well enough, all the blood and tongues and nails of it. But there was no tug between them. No heart that opened. There was one occasion where Marlowe and the young Master Shakespeare (another writer for the London stage) had a drunken contest in an alley behind Blackfriars. They agreed to fellate each other there, and the playwright who produced the most ejaculate would be declared winner. Master Shakespeare proved triumphant, giving Marlowe several mouthfuls of the stuff. And while the two admired each other well enough after that, no love ever bloomed. There was, in fact, only one man with whom Christopher Marlowe knew he would never be parted. And being the skilled diviner that he was, our Marlowe understood this man was not a proper body at all, but instead something more like the shadow of a shadow. Marlowe encountered him inside a dream. Red-caped Mephistopheles, that long-fingered devil, led the playwright deep into an earthy hole, and there Marlowe met a young man who looked very much like himself. Dark-haired and dark-eyed. A cleft upon his chin. The only difference between them was that this young man had a long-handled dagger sticking out of his right temple, silver blade thrust into his brain. Marlowe sat with the young man in the cave and they talked together. The playwright learned what it was like to be dead and murdered. And the young man learned what it was like to still be foolish and alive. At the end of a long night, the two—both no more than thirty years of age—fell asleep in each other's arms.

[Sleep] Endymion

Rome, 32 BCE

There are no memories here. Instead: a rose garden on a hill.

*

Dark vines clutch broken columns.

*

Blossoms swell like wounds.

*

To a young Greek shepherd, the hazy sprawl of Rome looks like the bright surface of a star. Endymion watches as slaves lead spotted leopards toward the amphitheater below. Tents are raised, fabric painted to match the color of the sky.

*

We must remind ourselves that Endymion is dreaming.

*

His body lies naked, far from Rome, in a vast Arcadian wood.

*

Moonlight steals across his sleeping form. Black beetles and silvery flies crawl in the curls of his hair. The shadow of a laurel tree darkens his upturned face. And, at least once a night, the faintest of breezes causes his cock to swell. His semen is a pearl dissolved.

*

Why has he slept so many years?

*

Such questions lead to circular paths.

*

Endymion turns his thoughts to the dark-haired youth, Aetes. The two young shepherds kissed often beneath the cover of the nighttime sky.

*

Aetes' lips... sweet like ripened dates.

*

Endymion runs his hand over the hairless swelling of Aetes' chest, moving his fingers along the young man's ribs, counting them. "You should have been an athlete," Endymion says.

Aetes laughs, but he does not look at Endymion. Instead, he gazes at the flock of sheep on the hill.

"I want to feel your skin against mine," Endymion says. "I want to feel you deeper too."

Aetes remains silent.

"What's wrong?"

"The sheep—" Aetes says.

"The sheep are fine."

Aetes lowers his head. Dark hair falls across his brow. "My father spoke to a family in Knossos," he says. "They are wealthy and have an unmarried daughter."

"Unmarried?"

"Yes," Aetes replies.

*

Cheers rise from the emperor's stadium. Gladiators slaughter leopards. Endymion hears the poor creatures' cries.

*

In his dream, Endymion walks the perimeter of the rose garden. Roman youths have scribbled graffiti on the walls: *The perfume maker fucked well here. My cock is dearer to me than life.*

*

A wind comes from the east. It lashes the heads of the roses.

*

Endymion closes his eyes. Aetes is there once more, wearing his shepherd's robes.

*

"Where have you been all these years?" Aetes asks.

"Sleeping," Endymion says. "I slept because of you."

"Because I left?" Aetes says. "Because I married?"

"Not only that," Endymion replies, thinking of painted murals in great houses. Bright pastorals. Wan shepherds, reclining on a hill. Such figures could never fall in love.

*

Another piece of graffiti: *Do not worry about the end of the world. The world has already ended.*

*

Endymion comes to the edge of the Roman garden. Beyond the wall are a series of tall white sepulchers, a burial ground for the Roman dead. He remembers the last night he spent with Aetes. In the morning, when the young shepherd stood to leave, the two could not meet each other's gaze.

*

Roses in the garden stare at Endymion now.

*

They have the red faces of the gods.

The Dogs

Here are the dogs, long-bodied and smooth, winding like serpents through the underbrush. They climb the trees and hang from branches. Some will sleep, but others stare. See the whites of their eyes? See their many teeth? Here are the dogs, silent as they are. And this is their kingdom, the forest. When they sleep, they dream of an ancient form, a hero. His fur is dark and rough with mud. His muzzle, flecked with foam. He walks alone because there is not yet another like him. And the dreaming dogs know the hero too must have dreamed. Perhaps he dreamed a dark crevasse, the entrance to some underworld. The hero crept down into the earth, into the pits and the bowels, and there he saw many things. The dead, for instance. Eyes like yellow stones. Mouths dry and grinning. He knew the dead would follow him. For the dead will always follow. So the hero quickened his step. And he saw the luminous flowers that grow beneath the earth. He saw cups of gold and cups of jewels. The hero whined in his sleep. Just as the dogs of the forest whine in their own sleep. Then the hero moved deeper still. And he saw the earth itself was full of bodies that were not like dogs. Bodies that had grown fat and full, having gorged themselves. The hero understood there are countries in dreams from which one can never quite fully return. It was a mistake to travel so deep. A mistake to look inside the earth. And when the dreaming dogs finally awake in the forest, do they forget their dreams? Yes, they forget their dreams as they slip along the paths toward the silent stone village beyond the trees. Night covers over everything still. The dogs, jaws open and tongues lolling, creep down empty cobbled streets. They want to eat. They want to eat.

The Sodomite

Milan, 1524

Il Sodoma (the Sodomite) paints in the open air of his courtyard.

He works in the morning and early evening. Hours when the sun is cool.

His paints are made from mineral: red iron and yellow clay, manganese and lime white.

He maintains, in his villa, an assortment of animals: badger, squirrel, jackdaw, a dwarf pony, an ape, and a turtle dove. The creatures are tame. They gambol and fly about as the artist paints.

Sodoma's most celebrated work is *The Martyrdom of Saint Sebastian*.

In the painting, the saint is handsome, naked, young. He is shown tethered to a tree that grows from a dark and fantastic landscape. His flesh is pierced by arrows. One arrow protrudes from Sebastian's sturdy neck, the other from his tensed thigh.

Sodoma uses two models to make his painting. One is called Blasio, a beardless youth from the village. Blasio is arrogant, thoughtless. He arrives late for his sittings and leaves the villa when he pleases. He speaks in a condescending manner, as if he thinks Sodoma is a feeble old man.

The other model is Luca, the stableman. Sodoma's sister, Antonia, believes Luca is an idiot. She claims he drools as he grooms the horses. Sodoma knows this is not true. Antonia is often cruel.

Sodoma speaks to the stableman as he paints. "Do you know the saint called Sebastian?" he asks.

"I do not, Sodoma," the stableman replies, attempting to remain as still as possible in the cool air of the courtyard. He is naked and strong. He stands with his hands held limply behind his back. His cock is thick, rope-like.

"He was martyred by the Romans," Sodoma says, dipping his horsehair brush in ochre-colored paint, studying the line of the stableman's shoulder. "Now, he protects men from the plague."

"Does he, Sodoma?" Luca asks.

"The saint was a young man when he died. Pierced by arrows."

"That would not be a good way to die," Luca says.

Sodoma rests his brush on the tray of the easel. "What if I told you I want to be pierced, Luca?"

The stableman raises his dark brow, perhaps surprised. But only mildly so, Sodoma thinks. "By arrows?" Luca asks.

"No," Sodoma says. "Not by arrows."

Luca's cock stiffens quickly enough. He penetrates Sodoma on the sofa in the great room of the villa. Yellow light falls through the high window. There are wildflowers in a vase near the sofa: foxglove, cowslip, daisies. The menagerie becomes restless. The jackdaw makes a sound like a winding clock. The ape paces back and forth beneath the window, glancing nervously from time to time at the men on the sofa.

As Luca thrusts, penetrating Sodoma, the artist walks in a garden, speaking to Saint Sebastian.

"Did you want to die for Christ?" Sodoma asks the handsome saint.

"I did not die," Sebastian says.

"You did," Sodoma replies. "You were pierced by arrows and then stoned. Martyred by Diocletian. All the histories tell it so."

"Old books lie," Sebastian says. "You should find something new to read."

On the sofa, Luca ejaculates inside Sodoma. The stableman's semen is like the egg white that Sodoma uses to mix his paints.

After Luca withdraws, he pauses. "Did I hurt you, Sodoma?" he says. "You are bleeding."

Sodoma reaches back and touches the opening where Luca so recently penetrated him. He brings his fingers forward and looks at the bright blood on his fingertips.

"No, Luca," Sodoma says then. "You did not hurt me at all."

How to Write a Ghost Story

Remember the first word you ever spoke. Now, write that word down on a piece of paper. What word did you write? Was it "ghost?" Good. That's a start. Now, think about why this was the first word you ever spoke. Was it because of what you saw in your bedroom that night? How old were you? Two years old? Three years old? Was it a dark shape? A shape that seemed to turn and dance? Good. Now, remember how you began to cry that night. You cried because you knew something was wrong. The shape that turned and danced did not belong in your room, and yet there it was. Now, remember how you saw the same dark shape later in life. You were a grown man the second time you saw it, nearly forty years old in fact. You were in bed alone. Your partner, Matthew, had recently left you, saying the two of you were different people. You still loved him though. And you couldn't believe he would use these imagined differences against you. You wondered if he had simply met someone else, someone more attractive or someone who was more interested in sex. Remember it was the middle of the night when you opened your eyes. You saw the dark shape turning and dancing in your room. Now, remember thinking the word "ghost." Remember thinking: "Shadow from another world." And then: "This is what I saw when I was two or three years old." Remember closing your eyes. Remember believing that, when you opened your eyes again, the dancing shape would be gone. Remember opening your eyes. See how the dancing shape is still there in the middle of your room? Good. Now, remember waiting in your bed, hoping the dancing would cease. Hoping the thing would dissolve or drift away. Remember how the thing did not dissolve or drift away but, instead, danced closer and closer to your bed. Remember how the thing was soon close enough that you could see more than just the dark outline of its body. Remember realizing the dancing thing had a face. The face was pink and fleshy, sick-looking. Its mouth hung open. It had tiny rounded teeth. Remember thinking: "This is not the face of a dead thing. This is the face of something that was never actually alive." Now, write down the word that means "something that was never actually alive." While you are writing, remember that you are not dreaming. You have never been dreaming all these forty years. Remember how the thing reaches out to touch you. Can you see how it dances still as it shows its little teeth? Good.

Saint Sebastian in Extremis

Each of my wounds is a mouth attempting to swallow a sword. I am tied to an alder tree, wrists bound. My lashings are made of Roman leather, knotted by soldiers I once called friends: Atilius, Gnaeus, Sabinus. Springtime blossoms burst from branches above my head. They too are wounds. Blood and sap mix. The bark of the alder tree shines.

In the prisons of Emperor Diocletian, I fell in love with two men, my cellmates: Marcellian, who was large and rough, a brute drawn from Attic tales. Imagine him horned, covered in the coarse hair of an animal. And then there was Marcus. He had a narrow face and thin-fingered hands. His body was like that of a moonlit figure in a burial yard. Each night, in the space of our small cell, I brought these men to Christ. I kissed their mouths and spread myself wide. My flesh, they said, was sweeter than any communion wine. More fortifying than any host. Together, we reinvented the trinity. A holy wheel aflame in the catacombs.

On the day of my execution, the sky was no color I could name. A wind blew from the North. The branches of the alder tree creaked above. My lovers were both murdered by the Romans. Dragged behind horses. Marcellian's jaw caught on a sharp rock. His head was pulled off. Marcus's red guts were strewn across the paving stones. Then the soldiers came to me. They bound my wrists. They took turns shooting arrows. They laughed and talked of other things. I gazed skyward. I thought of my youth, the services of my flesh. Doors opened in my skin. Each arrow was a kind of key. "Soon," I said softly, "the whole world will fit inside of me."

The Knight

A fragment recently discovered in the erotic collections of the Chevalier de Lorraine.

...and desperate as I was, I followed him, careful to remain hidden and always at some remove. He travelled north along a forgotten road to a pine forest that lay in the shadow of an ancient city on a hill. The knight, tall and pale upon his mount, dressed in armor that looked as though it had been carved for him from bone. He moved in decorous silence, hair as black as a walnut tree and body, broad and strong. I'd heard in local taverns that knights, in their brotherhoods, were more naturally disposed to predilections such as mine. On long and difficult journeys, such men became steeped in the brew of their own manhood. There were tales of ritual passions. The Hospitallers of Saint John, lost in a fog for days, were said to have fallen into convulsions of lust. Men with red crosses painted on bare chests, writhing together on the forest floor. A great howl rose from them when they found release, loud enough, it was said, to polish the very rim of Heaven.

And so, I followed the knight, not yet brave enough to betray my own existence, but wanting from him whatever he would give. When he climbed the worn and broken steps of the marble city on the hill, I too ascended. And passing through the city's gates, I found its streets empty and thought some plague might have ravaged its populace as had happened some years ago to the cities in the West. The knight himself seemed unmoved and rode through the narrow streets at a steady pace.

I lost track of him in the maze of the empty city and searched for nearly an hour through winding thoroughfares and dim-lit alleyways where blighted grass grew up through broken cobbles. In the courtyard of what might have once been a palace, I passed statues so deformed by time they appeared to represent no human figure at all. And as shadows lengthened, the city started to seem as though it was not actually a city. The towers and temples were no more than shapes painted on a scrim. What lay beyond the scrim was impossible to know. And yet, I sensed it was something cold. Something that did not care for the passions of men. I tried to put such thoughts aside, reminding myself I wanted nothing more than to find the knight, to see if he might be persuaded to take interest in a lowly creature such as me.

By the time I spotted his dappled horse tied to a post outside what might have once served as a temple, dusk had fallen. Carefully, I approached the temple's narrow window, imagining what I might say to a valiant man like the knight: *Sir, I've come to the city because I lost my way. Sir, I wonder if you might—*

But what I saw through the window silenced all such thoughts. For the knight had removed his armor and mail and laid himself out on a stone bier, entirely naked. The fading light that fell through the narrow window made the sinews of his body look as if they were carved from stone. And his cock itself, resting in a thatch of dark hair, looked as if it had fallen into some enchanted sleep.

I entered the temple and went to the bier. The knight did not open his eyes as I approached. He did not even appear to breathe.

I waited there above him, studying his powerful body in silence. Then, I found I could not resist. I made as if to stroke his muscled chest. But I did not dare to actually touch him. I merely moved the air above his flesh, hoping he might awake and grab me, pull me down upon him with all his force.

Yet the knight did not stir, so I grew bolder. I put my mouth near his own mouth and kissed the air over his firm-looking lips once and then again. The knight remained silent and still.

Then, I looked down the bier toward his member, that pale and slumbering root.

I went to it and leaned forward, almost kissing the flesh of his manhood. I imagined myself nursing from it, taking whatever bright sap the knight held inside his body into my mouth.

And it was then, as I imagined the taste of his fluids, that I heard the shuffle of boots at the entrance of the temple.

I turned and saw the knight himself standing behind me at the door. He looked weary and much older than I'd first believed. And yet, he was the same man who lay upon the bier. The same long and handsome face. The same strong form. I knew he'd likely watched as I kissed the air above his prick.

I took a step away from him, for I was frightened, believing he might be some black magician.

The knight seemed to speak then in the city that was not a city, and though I heard no words, an odd notion entered me as a devil might enter a soul—*life takes many forms, but so, in turn, does death…*

The Cornfield

Ohio, 1994

Tom is in a cornfield. It is his father's cornfield. Prior to his father, the field belonged to Tom's grandfather. And before that, it belonged to Tom's great-grandfather who came to Ohio from Illinois after a flood.

Tom doesn't want to inherit the cornfield. To own a cornfield is to have children, to go to church, to join a bowling league. To own a cornfield is to have a wife. Tom doesn't want any of those things. Instead, he wants to have sex with men.

Tom thinks about having sex with men almost all the time. He thinks about it in Algebra class and while driving to work and before falling asleep at night. And though Tom understands he will likely never have sex with a man, he still does not want to own a cornfield. To own a cornfield would mean defeat.

Tom walks alone down one of the field's leafy rows. He pretends the row is a hallway in an old mansion. Tom sometimes reads ghost stories to forget about cornfields and the small Ohio town where he lives. He wishes he could lose himself in an old mansion from one of the stories now.

Losing himself wouldn't feel like death, Tom thinks. It would feel like escape.

Tom walks for a long time. And eventually, he comes to a worn-looking door in the cornfield. The door doesn't stand upright like other doors. Instead, it lies flat on the ground between the leafy rows.

At first, Tom thinks someone must have thrown the door into the field. Someone who was remodeling a house, perhaps. Someone who needed to get rid of a door.

Or maybe the door is a piece of an old house that once stood in the cornfield. Tom's father told him pieces of old houses sometimes surface in the fields: wash basins, broken china, coal stoves.

Soil, when tilled, can behave like water. Debris floats up from the bottom.

Tom wonders what would happen if he opened the door in the cornfield.

Maybe he would find a hallway beneath. Maybe the hallway would be lit by candlelight. Tom would meet a young man there, the kind of young man who might own a house in a ghost story. The young man would give Tom a tour of the house and tell him about all its ghosts. At the end of the tour, in a darkened parlor, the young man would kiss Tom's mouth. Then, he would unbutton Tom's shirt and kiss Tom's chest. He would move to unbutton the fly of Tom's jeans.

Tom reaches down and touches the rusty knob of the door.

He turns the knob and pulls.

The door doesn't open, but rather moves slightly to the left. Tom drags the door, revealing nothing but wet soil beneath. There are several pink earthworms on the surface of the soil. Tom sits on the ground beside the door. He understands, of course, that he already owns this cornfield. He owns the door as well. Tom puts his fingers in the earth and feels how damp it is and how cold.

A Description of My House

1.

In order to understand my house, you must imagine you've fallen in love.

2.

You met the man you are in love with at a party. When you saw him, you paused, thinking he looked like someone you knew. A boy you went to school with, perhaps. But you don't have a clear memory of this boy.

3.

In order to understand your beloved, you must remember your reoccurring dream. In your dream, you walk into a room and think: *I know this room. This is a room in my parents' house.* But when you awake, you know very well it was a not a room in your parents' house. It was some invented room. A place you'd never seen before.

4.

That's how it was with this man at the party. You felt as though you knew him, and yet, at the same time, you understood you might soon wake up and realize you didn't know him at all.

5.

Now, imagine this man you are in love with calls you one evening and invites you to go to another party. He says the party will be held in a forest near his house. The man says you will both need to wear costumes for the party. At first, you imagine dressing as a figure from history or a character in a film. But the man says those kinds of costumes would not be appropriate.

6.

When you arrive at the man's house, he produces a long piece of black fabric. You are to drape the black fabric over your head. The man says everyone at the party will wear pieces of fabric in just the same manner. And so, because you are in love, you drape the piece of black fabric over your head. You can see through the fabric because it is sheer. You watch as the man also drapes a piece of black fabric over his own head.

7.

The man takes you into the forest. You walk together between the trees, holding hands through the long black shrouds. There is no path. You must pick your way over the bramble. You ask how far you'll have to walk before you arrive at the party. The man says the party is not much farther. In fact, it's just up ahead. You keep walking. You wonder how large the forest is. You begin to think about how trees once covered most of the earth. You don't know why you have this thought. It merely passes through your mind as thoughts so often do. Soon, you are imagining prehistoric animals roaming amongst the trees. The creatures call to one another in the darkness. Then, you begin to think about how, before there were forests, the earth was covered entirely in water. You wonder what came before the water. It must have been some sort of gas, you decide.

8.

You imagine the gas that covered the earth. It shifts and turns, a great shadowy sea.

9.

You wonder if something like souls floated in the shadows of the sea.

10.

In the forest, you come to a clearing. You see shapes dancing around a fire. The shapes are bodies covered in dark fabric. They laugh and crouch. Sometimes they tremble, as if in anticipation of some important event. Your beloved takes your hand. He attempts to lead you toward the fire. "This is the party I told you about," he says. But instead of following, you pause. You look up.

11.

There, on a hill above the forest, is a house. This is *my* house. The one I've been telling you about. The door of my house is closed. The lights are off, and the windows are all dark. You think: *I know that house. I'm sure of it. I've seen it somewhere before.* But I can assure you you're wrong about that. You've never seen my house. And, in fact, you aren't seeing it now. You should go ahead into the clearing. Follow the man you're in love with and dance with the other guests around the fire.

Speaker at the Funeral

Only a few of us are in attendance. It is Wednesday, raining. Not a good day to go outside.

The deceased is called Robert. He is laid out in his coffin at the front of the chapel. He wears a faded suit. His hair is combed in thick grooved lines.

Robert worked with us at the factory. He manned the lathe and rarely spoke. The edges of his mouth were often downturned. Robert had no wife or children. Sometimes, he fell asleep while sitting in a chair in the small room where we ate our dinner. One of us joked once about the dull sort of dreams Robert must have. Everyone laughed.

At the beginning of the funeral, a man in a dark coat approaches the lectern. The man is bearded, long-fingered. We do not recognize him. Yet we understand he is meant to introduce the speaker.

We wonder why Deacon Bradford is not at the church. Deacon Bradford is a friendly man who always has a good word. He often asks us about our wives and children. Normally, the deacon introduces the speaker at a funeral. But, today, we do not see him.

The man in the dark coat removes a sheaf of papers from his pocket. He spreads the papers on the lectern. Then he lights a candle. The flame flickers dimly.

The man in the dark coat speaks, not to us, but to the floor. Most of what he says we cannot hear. There is one phrase, however: *This is the night of the world.* The man repeats the phrase several times. We do not know what to make of such a phrase. And we wish Deacon Bradford was in the chapel to interpret the words for us.

When the man in the dark coat is finished speaking, he folds his papers and returns them to his pocket. He steps down from the lectern and sits in a pew near the front of the chapel.

We wait for the speaker then. There is always a speaker at a funeral, someone who pays tribute to the dead. Surely, there will even be a man willing to pay tribute to Robert.

But, today, no such speaker appears.

We wonder if there's been some mistake.

We look at the man in the dark coat for an answer. But he merely sits in his pew, staring down at his long-fingered hands.

Finally, a door opens at the rear of the chapel. This is the door that leads to Deacon Bradford's office. We find ourselves relieved. Deacon Bradford will come and say cheerful things. Even at funerals, he is cheerful. But it is not the deacon who emerges from the office. It is the speaker.

The speaker is a woman. She's tall and broadly shaped. She wears a long dress made of yellowed lace. We have all seen our grandmothers and great-grandmothers wearing such dresses in old pictures. The speaker also wears a wide hat. There is no veil attached. And yet, for some reason, we cannot clearly see the speaker's face. We see nothing in the manner of eyes or a nose. We see a mouth, however, the lips of which are pulled tight. There are teeth under those lips. Yet we do not know the shape of the teeth.

The speaker walks slowly to the lectern and appears to gaze out at us with her eyeless face. Light from the candle shines on her sallow skin. And we wonder how this woman knew Robert.

We wait for the speaker's words.

But the speaker only stares at us.

When the words finally come, the speaker seems already to be in the middle of her intended talk. Perhaps she has been speaking quietly all along. Perhaps, we simply could not hear her.

The speaker does not seem to be talking about Robert. But then again, we cannot be sure. For as soon as she utters her words, they seem to fall away, slipping through cracks in the wooden floor of the church. We strain to catch the words before they fall. But we find we cannot.

Soon, we begin to feel we are no longer in the chapel.

Instead, we are in a dark cave. Stony walls surround us.

We feel we are moving toward a grim light at the mouth of the cave.

We walk out of the cave and see a vague landscape. The land is not made of earth. It is made of bodies. The bodies are all similar to that of the speaker. All of the bodies are dressed in yellowed lace. They are laid side by side in such a way as to form fields and low rolling hills.

We step out of the cave and into the landscape.

In order to walk, we must tread on bodies. We walk on lace and pallid skin. We walk on chests and closed mouths.

We see, in the distance, a tower.

The tower too is made of bodies. The bodies are all without eyes. All covered in lace. They are stacked, one upon the next, to form the floors and walls of the tower.

We walk slowly.

We enter the tower through an arched door made of bodies, and we see a staircase, also made of bodies.

We ascend the staircase and find a room that contains machines like the machines in our own factory. Here is the milling machine and the gear shaper. Here is the hone and even the lathe where Robert himself used to sit.

We realize none of the machines in the tower are composed of metal and wood like the ones in our factory. These machines are made of bodies, all dressed in yellowed lace. The bodies are crouched and contorted. Arms and legs become racks and treadles. Fingers are levers, and mouths are holes for milling. All the while, the figures who pretend to be machines stare at us with eyeless faces.

We take a step back. We want to run down the tower stairs, to return to the cave. But something holds us in place. Perhaps it is the gaze of the figures. We look at one another in the tower room, wishing Deacon Bradford was here with us to explain. Then we think of Robert working quietly at his lathe. We think of his downturned mouth. We think: *This is the night of the world.* And we wonder if Robert knew the meaning of such a phrase.

We approach the machines that are made of bodies. We study the figures, crouched in their yellowed dresses, pretending to be things they are not.

The figures breathe quietly.

They watch, waiting for us to begin our work.

Bones of Silver, Flesh of Gold

Lindau, Germany, 1846

1.

We knew the old philosophies, the air of death about them.

2.

Christians had ruined the finer gods, forced those spirits down from the mountains, driven them into broken temples and haunted groves.

3.

Our minds were like a blotting book. We loved the past, the great grim palaces and airy castles.

4.

And yet, when Albrecht Mueller arrived in the fullness of his youth, *he* was all we could think of. The pallid length of him. And hair so thick and dark.

5.

Each day, Herr Mueller rowed his father's boat onto the lake. And we watched him from the village. His lithe shoulders, his broad strokes. When he reached the lake's center, Herr Mueller stowed his oars and read from a slim volume. Poetry, we thought. Though we could not be sure. His vessel drifted. He turned pages. He did not look toward the village.

7.

In the evening hours, when he went walking, we asked Herr Mueller the name of the volume that he read. He smiled at us, a young man's smile, and said the names of his books were not important. We would not be interested. For we had our work, after all. And our good families.

8.

Herr Mueller, with his cold white limbs.

9.

One evening, when he was some seventeen years of age and drunk from black ale, he forgot his book on a table in the tavern. We collected it, as if it was some artifact meant for a reliquary. What we saw when we lifted its cover filled us with disappointment. For the book was just as Herr Mueller had suggested, a collection of poems from some unremarkable poet, an imitator of Schiller by the look of it. The words did not interest us, nor did the sentiments.

10.

And yet, was it ever the books that had drawn our attentions? Wasn't it, instead, Herr Mueller himself? Physical locus of some metaphysical agent.

11.

Bones of silver, flesh of gold.

12.

And so, what did we do? We are not proud of our actions. We bid Herr Mueller's father to compel the boy to work. We said the mill lacked men. This was, of course, a lie. The mill had never lacked men. Yet, Herr Mueller's father, being a good member of our society, complied with our wishes. Young Herr Mueller himself did not complain. He arrived at the mill in workman's clothes. He labored at our side and spoke to us. Always at some remove, but still, he spoke.

13.

At evening time, Herr Mueller, covered in the dust of the mill, dragged his father's boat to the edge of the lake and hoisted his oars, taking himself once more to its center. But he did not read a book of poetry there. For it was too dark for that. Herr Mueller merely sat in his rowboat long after we ourselves had gone to bed. We always went to bed early for we knew we must wake with the dawn.

14.

It was on one such early morning we found the boat, empty, drifting. And, of course, we understood what we had done.

15.

When we saw Herr Mueller in his coffin, flesh powdered and cheeks rouged, we knew he still held within him certain secrets. Lines that could never be written in any book of poetry. And we longed to follow him into the ground. To beg him to act as our guide in the silent places of the earth.

16.

But we could not go where he was called. For that is how it is with gods.

Let Us Go and Serve Other Gods

Deuteronomy 13: 6-10

"If thy brother, or thy son, or the wife of thy bosom, or thy friend entice thee secretly, saying, 'Let us go and serve other gods,' thou shalt not consent unto him. Do not hearken unto him. Thine hand shall be first upon him. And thou shalt stone him with stones, that he die. (But even as the first stone is cast, you will think perhaps: *Where might we find these other gods?* For haven't you always wondered such things when you were alone in the silence of your rooms? So, let me show you now. Let me show you. Follow me into this dark fissure, this narrow wound in the earth. Follow me down past the places where the dead are buried. See how they are laid out, arms crossed, flowers pressed to the hollows of their eyes. See how they rest in the rooms of towers that do not rise but rather travel further into the earth. See the plague pits here with their death parades. Corpses dressed in florid silk. See the coffins made of marble and brass and ivory. Then, beneath these newly dead, see the bones of the old beasts that once walked the earth when the sky was dim and black stars hung closer than the moon. Listen to the sounds the old stars made as they turned. Follow me down, deeper still. See the buried pyramids and ziggurats, mastabas and painted caves. Here there are circles drawn in the earth. Here there are remnants of the first garden. Ferns pressed beneath the weight of stones. Pits of old fruit, scattered. We are deeper now. Yet we must travel further. Trailing the empty corridors of silver ships that once sailed the darkness before there was land or water or even light. We nod to the old sailors resting in their cabins, long-fingered men with odd black eyes, dressed in collars of emerald and gold. And on we travel, until it seems as if there will soon be no earth left to plumb. Perhaps we grow tired. We lie down and close our eyes. And, as we fall asleep, our bodies slide on loose pebbles, moving us into deeper caverns. We come to rest on the floor of an old house made of neither wood nor stone. We do not see the occupants of the house because we are still asleep. And these occupants step quietly around our heads, careful not to wake us. We ask ourselves [because we have traveled so far and because we have left so much behind] are these the other gods then? Have we finally found them? We ask these questions in our dreams, even as the figures kneel down to kiss us on our mouths, to stroke our cheeks with timeworn hands, to show us we have always been loved)."

Acknowledgments

My extreme gratitude to Diane Goettel and everyone at Black Lawrence Press for believing in this collection and bringing it into the world. Thank you also to my thoughtful and diligent agent Eleanor Jackson who has provided invaluable guidance over our years of working together. I'd also like to extend thanks to my colleagues and students at Vermont College of Fine Arts and the University of California Los Angeles Extension Program, all of whom consistently remind me of the wide and dynamic range of possibilities in fiction. Thank you to Brian Leung for reading many drafts of my work over the years and responding with intelligence, humor, and compassion. For their help with my writing and for their friendship, I'd like to thank Chris Baugh, Christine Sneed, Scott Blindauer, and Gabriel Blackwell. Thank you also to my supportive mother and father, Denise and Michael, and my sisters, Sarah and Elizabeth. And finally, thank you to my partner, the handsome, musically gifted, and funny Brad Beasley for his encouragement and love. He makes every moment feel special.

Thanks to the editors of the publications in which the following stories first appeared:

Always Crashing: "The Maze"
Atticus Review: "A Roman Road", "Genesis"
The Collagist: "A Memory of the Christ by the Apostle John"
Bateau: "Saint Sebastian in Extremis"
Black Warrior Review: "Loup-Garou"
Café Irreal: "Man with Pillow"
Clockhouse: "A Description of My House"
Coffin Bell: "Wolves Can Be Mistaken"
Columbia: "[Sleep] Endymion"
Crab Orchard Review: "Plumed and Armored, We Came"
Diagram: "On Decadence", "Notes on the Heavens"
Ghost City: "The Cornfield"
Grimoire: "A Horror", "An Orgy"
Hobart Pulp: "It's Later Than You Think"
Juked: "Gilgamesh and Enkidu"
New South: "For Witches"
OxMag: "How to Write a Ghost Story"
Orca: "Let Us Go and Serve Other Gods"
The Portland Review: "The Coil"
Queen Mob's Tea House: "Mars, 1887"
Ruminate: "The Pool Party"
The Rupture: "There's Someone at the Door"
Salt Hill: "Deep in the Hundred Acre Wood"
Sonora Review: "The Pleasure Garden"
Third Point Press: "The Dogs"
Tilde: "Marlowe in Love"
The Tiny Journal: "Speaker at the Funeral"
Vestiges: "Pan and Hook"
Wigleaf: "Fantasy Kit/1942"

Photo: Rebecca Johnson

Adam McOmber is the author of three novels, *The White Forest*, *Jesus and John*, and *The Ghost Finders*, as well as two previous collections of short stories: *My House Gathers Desires* and *This New & Poisonous Air*. His queer retelling of Arthur Conan Doyle's *The Hound of the Baskervilles* is forthcoming from Lethe Press in October 2022. He is a core faculty member in the Writing Program at Vermont College of Fine Arts as well as editor-in-chief of the literary magazine *Hunger Mountain*.

www.ingramcontent.com/pod-product-compliance
Lightning Source LLC
Chambersburg PA
CBHW020321030826
48979CB00022B/656

* 9 7 8 1 6 2 5 5 7 1 4 0 3 *